"Thank you for last night," Laney said.

"But I don't want what happened to affect our friendship—or the boys' relationship. You're the best friend I've ever had and I don't want the fact that we've had sex to ruin that."

Ben gazed down at the tousled silk of her hair and the flushed skin of her shoulders in disbelief. She actually thought he'd slept with her just to be nice! He wanted to be with her always. To be a real father to Josh.

Maybe he was pushing things too fast and Laney was too upset over Reese's betrayal and murder to even consider committing herself to another relationship.

"Nothing's changed since yesterday," he said finally. "You can always count on our friendship. I don't fly across the country for just anyone—just you."

The slight trembling of her jaw confirmed his suspicions. She wasn't unaffected by their lovemaking. Just not ready. Well, he could respect that. And he could wait.

ABOUT THE AUTHOR

Joyce credits her lawyer mother with instilling in her a love of reading and writing—and a fascination for solving mysteries. She has a bachelor's degree in criminal justice and worked several years as a private investigator before turning her hand to writing romantic suspense. A transplanted American, Joyce makes her home in Aylmer, Quebec, with her handsome French-Canadian husband and two casebook-toting kid detectives.

Books by Joyce Sullivan

HARLEQUIN INTRIGUE
352—THE NIGHT BEFORE CHRISTMAS
436—THIS LITTLE BABY

To Laney, With Love
Joyce Sullivan

To the Patrons of the Aylmer Library,

Hope you enjoy Ben & Laney's story.

Joyce Sullivan

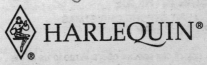

HARLEQUIN®

TORONTO • NEW YORK • LONDON
AMSTERDAM • PARIS • SYDNEY • HAMBURG
STOCKHOLM • ATHENS • TOKYO • MILAN • MADRID
PRAGUE • WARSAW • BUDAPEST • AUCKLAND

ISBN 0-373-22516-4

TO LANEY, WITH LOVE

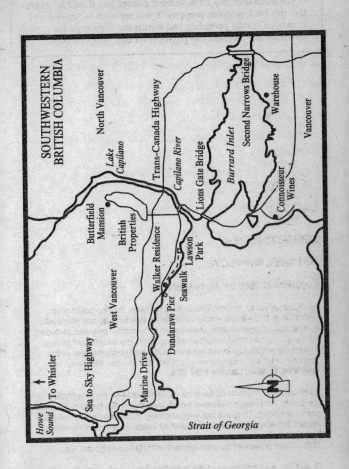

SOUTHWESTERN BRITISH COLUMBIA

Howe Sound

To Whistler

Sea to Sky Highway

West Vancouver

Butterfield Mansion

British Properties

Lake Capilano

North Vancouver

Trans-Canada Highway

Capilano River

Lions Gate Bridge

Burrard Inlet

Second Narrows Bridge

Warehouse

Vancouver

Connoisseur Wines

Marine Drive

Dundarave Pier

Seawalk

Walker Residence

Lawson Park

Strait of Georgia

N

CAST OF CHARACTERS

Laney Dobson—Was she or wasn't she a widow?

Ben Forbes—He loved Laney, but his personal code of ethics wouldn't allow him to romance another man's wife.

Reese Dobson—How could a dead man send a Valentine?

Graham Walker—He was a dead ringer for Reese.

Kristel Walker—How much did she know about her husband's life?

Nelson Butterfield—He'd do anything to protect his sister Kristel.

Yale Sheridan—He had a reputation worth millions to protect.

Dallyn Vohringer—He and Graham Walker had an interesting partnership.

Colombe Cyr—This child psychologist was Laney's close friend and confidante.

Ivan and Rico—Who did these hoodlums work for?

Scott Forbes and Josh Dobson—They were best friends who wanted to be brothers.

Chapter One

To Laney, With Love.

The familiar handwriting on the small, stiff white envelope she'd found tucked into her mailbox on her wedding anniversary made Laney Dobson's heart palpitate. The advertising circulars dropped with a thunk to the snow-encrusted front step as she pulled off her fur-lined leather gloves and slid trembling fingers beneath the back flap of the envelope. The frigid Ottawa temperature numbed her fingers to the bone as she pulled out a beautifully ornate Victorian card that depicted a youthful, dark-haired rapscallion snatching a kiss from a rosy-cheeked, blue-eyed maiden.

Laney fearfully opened the card. Written plain as day were a few lines in her husband's hand:

Love is a mystery that can't be explained.
The harder one tries, the more hopelessly tangled one becomes.
Never doubt you're my one and only, Laney.

R.

Laney shook her head, trying to rouse herself from what could only be a dream. Reese, her husband, was dead.

The cold nipping her cheeks convinced her she wasn't asleep and she wasn't imagining the note. Forgetting the circulars, she opened the door of her sun porch and made a hectic dash back into the foyer of her house, needing to feel the security of the walls of the cozy cottage she'd shared with Reese for the nine years they'd been married, around her. The card and the envelope were still in her hands when she dared to look at them again. The writing still resembled Reese's.

Laney sagged against the wall, bumping into Josh's hockey stick, which poked out from the umbrella stand of her oak hall tree. Hope flared in her heart. Reese's body had never been recovered from the avalanche in the coastal mountains of Whistler, British Columbia. Could he have survived somehow?

Why wait fourteen months to contact her, then?

Laney examined the envelope. There was no postmark. It had been hand-delivered. Today was Monday. She'd been home working all morning. She and Josh had been in and out over the weekend for his hockey games Saturday and Sunday morning, followed by a family skating party for the team Sunday afternoon.

They'd been so busy she'd forgotten to get the Sunday circulars from the mailbox. But she couldn't believe Reese would come by the house and not let himself in. A spare key for Josh was still hidden inside a grinning verdigris frog strategically placed on a boulder in the shrub bed to the left of the front steps. At least she thought so. She stumbled outdoors to check. The key was still in the frog, right where it should be. Reese couldn't possibly have delivered the note. If he were alive, he'd be here with them.

So who had?

Josh?

The answer was so simple that Laney scolded herself as tears sprang to her eyes. He and his friend Scott had been rummaging through the boxes in the basement for clothes to conceal their superhero costumes. Maybe they'd found the card in one of Reese's coat pockets—Reese had always been romantic about planting love notes in unexpected places—and Josh had decided to give it to her. It was sweet and thoughtful.... He'd probably tucked it in the mailbox before leaving for school this morning.

Laney choked back a sob. Good thing Josh hadn't been here when she'd discovered it, because her blubbering would probably have upset him. Josh was the most wonderful gift Reese had ever given her. It broke her heart that her little boy was going to grow up without a father. Laney lovingly pressed the card to her lips and stood it on the glove box of the hall tree so Josh would know she'd found it. Then, heading outside, she wiped her damp cheeks to prevent her tears from forming into icicles while she scraped the frost off her car windows.

If she didn't hurry she'd be late for a planning meeting at Carleton University, where she worked as a line editor for the university press.

"Heavens, you look terrible," Colombe Cyr proclaimed twenty minutes later when Laney barreled into the meeting room, hefting her leather satchel.

"Oh, thanks," Laney said, flashing the tall, silver-haired child psychologist a harried smile. Colombe was here on sabbatical from Dalhousie University in Halifax, working on a joint research project with a Carleton University child psychologist on the challenges of parenting blended families. They were in the midst of putting the final manuscript together. Laney had hit it off right away with the quirky Haligonian prof when they'd met almost a year ago. The fact they were both widows gave them an immediate empathy for each other. "I'm racing as usual. Are we still on for lunch? In between the gossip, I want to pick your brain about something personal."

"Sounds interesting. Is it male-related?" Colombe grinned behind narrow, raspberry-pink eyeglass frames that softened the innately inquisitive sharpness of her owlish brown eyes.

"Sort of—it's about Josh." Actually, Laney hoped to solicit her friend's advice about how Josh was coping with Reese's death.

"Ah, one of my favorite males. I'm all ears. How about the Faculty Club? I feel like celebrating. We're almost done with the project."

Laney smiled, glad she wouldn't have to lunch alone on her wedding anniversary. She could raise a glass of wine and toast Reese.

VALENTINE'S DAY was two weeks away. Ben Forbes looked at his day planner on his desk and tried to figure out what sticky rules of etiquette applied when a man wanted to ask out the mother of his son's best friend. After his wife Rebecca had died of breast cancer four years ago, he'd had his fair share of dates since returning to the singles scene. Why did this one make him so nervous?

He knew exactly why. Because it was Laney. He'd never met a woman whose personality sparkled so brilliantly in her eyes. Those blue eyes danced with animation when she spoke. When she smiled, his heart spun like a puck on ice, and the sound of her musical laugh was enough to make him want to grovel at her feet.

And her body…oh, God! Every cell of Ben's body went rigid at the thought. Laney's soft, curvaceous body was a vessel for joy and Ben anticipated each minute he'd spend in her company like a teenager in the throes of his first crush.

The truth was, he'd been in love with her since two days before Christmas. She'd helped the boys bake sugar cookie angels, which the boys had then tied to helium balloons that Laney had bought to send their homemade gifts heavenward to Josh's dad and Scott's mom. Ben would never forget the joy on his son's face when Laney had given Scott a permanent marker so he could write a message to his mom on the balloon. He'd written, "I love you. I'm on the Olympics hockey team this year. Dad's the best coach."

Ben swallowed hard and wiped away the moisture forming in his eyes. Laney had given Scott his mom back. She'd opened a connection that felt real to Scott. Ben would have given anything for a bough of mistletoe just then so he'd have an excuse to see if

Laney's kisses were as warm and fiery as the auburn of her hair. He'd settled for slipping his arm around her waist and drawing her close to him as they'd watched the yellow balloons ascend toward the heavens. He'd vowed right there and then that somehow, some way, the Dobsons and the Forbeses were going to become a family.

Ben scowled at the calendar. If the information from a nine-year-old informant—Laney's son—could be believed, Laney hadn't dated at all since Reese's death. Was Valentine's Day too soon? Maybe he should wait until the boys' hockey season was over.

If Laney turned him down, they'd both be spared the awkwardness of avoiding each other in the change rooms before and after the Olympics' games. Not that they wouldn't have to see each other when the boys played together after school and on weekends. Scott had spent the night at Laney's house last weekend. Ben had shared a cup of coffee with her Sunday morning while the boys finished blueberry pancakes and scurried downstairs to the basement to put on their hockey gear, chattering excitedly.

Lord, it had been sheer bliss. The only thing that could have made it better would have been to wake up beside her and thoroughly love every inch of her creamy skin before breakfast.

Ben gripped his pen so tightly his fingers cramped. No, he couldn't wait until the end of the season. It had to be Valentine's Day. Laney had a romantic streak. Her house was filled with flowers and bows and hand-painted china. Not to mention the pieces of art that Reese had brought her as gifts from his travels all over the world working as a financial analyst for CDN Investments. Reese had been Mr. Romance, apparently. Ben had learned that last October when he'd fixed a leaky tap in the master bathroom suite Reese had given Laney one Valentine's Day. The tub had a waterfall, for Pete's sake, plus a bank of mirrors and enough candles to light a church.

But what did a civil engineer who dealt in waste management know about romance—beyond the obligatory bouquet of roses? He and Rebecca had met in university. She'd been an engineer, too. Romance to them had been a six-pack of beer and a pizza. Laney was accustomed to a higher standard.

Ben sighed and kneaded his brow. Whatever he did, it had to be good.

JOSH HAD DONE IT AGAIN. Laney stared at the pink envelope in her mailbox, addressed in Reese's handwriting, and wondered if her son had found a stash of Reese's notes in the basement. But why today, the fifth of February?

Was Josh worried because she'd blown a fuse when he'd dropped the pitcher of orange juice on the kitchen floor at breakfast? The day had gotten off to a bad start. She'd stayed up way too late the night before line-editing a manuscript and didn't hear the music on her radio-alarm clock for a good twenty minutes this morning. In the frantic race to mop the floor and pack his lunch, she'd realized she'd forgotten to buy granola bars for Josh's lunch box. How could the lack of chocolate-coated oatmeal ruin a kid's day? Probably for the same inexplicable reason that her day had soured when Josh announced he couldn't find one of his mittens. Her lecture that he needed to be more responsible for his belongings earned her a guilt-inducing, "Scott's dad is a single parent and he never yells at Scott for dumb things like losing a mitten."

Laney sighed. Ben Forbes was perfect in Josh's eyes. To be honest, Ben Forbes was perfect in just about any woman's eyes and he had the social life to prove it. Sleek black hair, heartbreaker blue-black eyes and a wide, generous smile that she was finding increasingly hard to ignore. No wonder he was the buzz of minor-league hockey. And he was wonderful with the kids. Especially Josh. Josh was the only kid on the team whose dad wasn't around—at least occasionally—to lace up his hockey skates. Laney just didn't have the right touch. Josh always complained his skates were never tight enough when she did them. But they were perfect when Ben laced them.

It was one of those mysterious rites of boyhood that Laney didn't understand. She was just glad Ben didn't mind helping out.

Laney tore open the envelope and found a gilded, peephole valentine. Unease fluttered in her stomach when she saw the slumbering cupid framed in a vibrant red, heart-shaped border. With hesitant fingers, she lifted the top flap of the card. The cupid lay on a bed of white satin strewn with flowers, reminding her morbidly of the pink, red and yellow roses she'd thrown into the crevasse where Reese lay buried beneath three hundred feet of snow.

Her throat tightened convulsively as she read Reese's words:

To Laney, with love
From your one and only Valentine
I know you have questions but I can explain
The Rendezvous 1:00 p.m. Christine's.
Whistler, Valentine's Day.
Make this our little secret. No police.

R.

Laney swayed and gripped the wooden railing as her knees gave out. Her thoughts alternated between disbelief and shock. This couldn't be happening...there must be some mistake. How could he be alive? She scanned the message again, her hand trembling so badly she could hardly read. "Make this our little secret" and "No police" conveyed a sinister, illicit context that made her stomach churn.

Laney sank onto the wooden steps and laid the card in her lap. Her head swam with confusing thoughts. Had Reese delivered the other note on their wedding anniversary a couple of weeks ago? Josh hadn't said a word about the card she'd propped up on the hall tree. But then, he didn't like talking about his dad.

Anger cut a swath through the confusion swirling in her brain. How dare Reese do this to her and Josh! What possible explanation could justify putting her and Josh through the agony of thinking him dead? Not to mention the legalities. Her heart skittered around like a stone in her rib cage as she thought about the money she'd collected on Reese's life-insurance policy. Had she committed fraud?

Resting her head in her hands, Laney struggled between the temptation to call her lawyer and not go to Whistler at all, and her obligations to her wedding vows and to Josh.

The chill of the steps permeated the thick insulation of her coat and numbed the bones of her spine as the improbable story lines of various soap operas and TV-movies-of-the-week fueled a tenuous hope that her husband was about to be restored to her on the most romantic day of the year.

Maybe Reese had survived the avalanche and had been in a coma or suffered amnesia. Or maybe he'd witnessed a crime and the accident had been staged so he could be put into a witness protection program.

Or, a tiny voice pointed out, it was possible he'd used the avalanche as an excuse to walk away from them. He'd always been an independent man who'd needed his space. He traveled a great deal on business and often took a few days off to ski or golf, depending on the season. He always made time for a side trip to Whistler when he was in Vancouver on business. Now she wondered if his need for these solitary trips was an indication he wasn't happy in their marriage. Maybe deep down he'd felt pressured into marrying her because she was pregnant and the thrill of being in love and being a father had worn thin for him. Laney tried to quash the tiny doubting voice. She told herself that Reese loved her and their son.

Whatever the explanation, she realized she owed it to herself and to Josh to hear Reese out. Somehow she had to get to Whistler, British Columbia, for Valentine's Day—without Josh.

LANEY BREATHED A SIGH of relief when she arrived at Scott's house at five-thirty to pick up Josh for dinner and saw Ben's dark-green minivan in the driveway.

Laney rang the doorbell.

Georgina Forbes, Scott's grandmother, a trim, efficient woman in dove-gray slacks and a pastel pink sweater, answered the door, wiping her blue-veined hands on a colorful dish towel draped over her shoulder. Laney was sure Ben had inherited every nice bone in his body from his mother. Georgina watched Scott after school and often had dinner with her son and grandson before driving off to her apartment in Vanier. "Come in, Laney. I was just trying to get a brownie pudding in the oven for dessert. I'll tell Josh you're here."

Laney sniffed appreciatively. The house smelled heavenly of garlic, Italian spices and melted chocolate. The shouts and the monotonously merry music floating out from the living room told her the boys were happily occupied playing video games.

She gripped the valentine tucked into her coat pocket. "Wait, Georgina. Is Ben home? I was hoping I could talk to him privately for a minute."

Ben's mother's lips quirked into a crooked smile that lit up her thin face and her pale-gray eyes. "He's downstairs. He took the afternoon off and he's been locked in the basement working on a top-secret project. Feel free to enter at your own risk."

"Thanks." Laney slipped out of her fawn leather boots, but left her coat on. She made a quick detour into the living room where Josh and Scott sat side by side on the carpet in front of the TV. She ruffled Josh's blond hair.

"Aw, Mom, is it time to go already?" he complained. "I have a wedding to crash and a princess to save."

Laney tried to keep a straight face. So far, Josh and Scott had steered clear of girls. Video-game princesses were obviously excluded. "By all means, rescue the princess. I need to talk to Ben anyway."

"Good! Look out, I've got to kill the cake."

Scott tore his eyes away from a medieval-style iron-studded oak door that swung open to reveal a wedding chapel on the TV screen. His black eyes were characteristically solemn as he gave her a shy smile. "Good luck, Laney. Dad's grouchy. He wouldn't even let us practice shooting goals in the basement."

Just to be fair, she ruffled his hair, too. Scott's hair was the same midnight shade as Ben's, only curlier and saw a comb less often. "Thanks for the warning."

As she padded down the carpeted basement stairs in her socks, Laney could hear a slightly off-key male voice accompanying a song on the radio. Was that Ben? He didn't sound grouchy. His deep voice vibrated with contentment. Still, her legs trembled as she rapped on the closed door of his workshop. What was she going to do if he said no?

"Ben, it's Laney," she called in a shaky voice. "May I come in?"

Ben stopped singing in mid-verse and went into a full-scale panic as he dropped the rag he'd been using to stain the interlocking heart-shaped puzzle he'd spent the afternoon cutting and sanding from an oak plank. Laney was here?

"No! Hold on," he barked, stripping the latex gloves from his hands and shutting off the radio. "I'll be right out."

His heart hammered an uneven rhythm as he strode to the door and opened it, purposely blocking her view onto his workbench. His body reacted instantly as he took in the details of her pale face, the contrast of her auburn hair against her moss-green suede coat and the coral leggings clinging to her shapely legs.

"I—I'm sorry…" she stammered "…I could come back if this is a bad time."

Ben didn't know if it was the poor lighting in the basement, but he could swear he saw fear tainting her expressive eyes. Her hands were jammed into her pockets as though she was struggling to keep her composure.

He instinctively stepped toward her, closing the door behind him. "Now's fine. What's up?" he asked in concern, battling an urge to take her in his arms. "You look as if you've seen a ghost."

To his dismay, Laney blanched and swayed unsteadily on her feet. Ben grabbed her shoulders. The ultrafeminine feel of her limbs beneath her suede coat jolted his senses. "Easy! Do you want to sit down?"

Laney closed her eyes tightly for a second and shook her head. "No, I'd rather stand." Ben kept his hold on her just in case. "I need to ask you a favor."

"So ask," he said, knowing damn well he'd grant her anything for the glorious pleasure of being close enough to her to smell the tantalizingly tropical scent of her shampoo.

"I need to know if you can watch Josh for me for a few days next week," she said flatly. "I have to go out of town unexpectedly and I'm not sure exactly how long I'll be gone...."

A sense of impending doom hovered over his heart. *Next week?* "When are you leaving?" he croaked.

"I'm flying out on the thirteenth."

Great. Ben suffered a pang of disappointment as his hopes for a romantic Valentine's Day with Laney were reduced to a pile of sawdust. Just his luck a business trip would ruin his plans. Then he noticed the tears glimmering in her eyes.

He cupped her chin, nearly groaning aloud at the silky texture of her skin. Unbearable heat pounded to his groin. "Of course I'll take care of Josh, but where are you going? And why are you crying?"

A tear slipped onto her cheek as she pulled her right hand out of her pocket and thrust something at him, her voice brittle. "I'm going to see Reese. Apparently he's alive."

Shocked, Ben closed his fingers around the crumpled valentine clenched in her trembling fingers. His lungs burned from lack of oxygen as he unfolded the glitzy red card and read the message.

To Laney, with love
From your one and only Valentine
I know you have questions but I can explain
The Rendezvous, 1:00 p.m. Christine's
Whistler, Valentine's Day.
Make this our little secret. No police.

The knowledge Laney still belonged to another man paralyzed him. Ben drew a deep breath past the pain in his heart and tried to focus all his thoughts on the message in the card, which he didn't like the sound of one iota. Hell, Laney could be walking into a trap.

"How'd you get this?" he asked, examining the card carefully.

"I found it in my mailbox. There was no stamp or postmark." Her voice caught. From her left coat pocket she extracted a second card and opened it for him to see. "I got this one a couple of weeks ago, on our wedding anniversary."

Ben scanned the neatly block-printed words as she explained that she'd thought Josh had found it in the basement and put it in the mailbox to surprise her.

Love is a mystery that can't be explained.
The harder one tries, the more hopelessly tangled one becomes.
Never doubt you're my one and only, Laney.

R.

Ben swore under his breath. "Are you certain this is Reese's handwriting?"

Laney nodded. Two more giant tears squeezed

from her eyes. "How could he let us think he was dead?" She clamped her hand over her mouth, her whole body shaking.

"I don't know," he murmured thickly. Ben's heart tore into more pieces than the puzzle he'd made for her this afternoon. How could that jerk walk away from his wife and son? He'd always thought Reese was a selfish bastard, leaving Laney at home with their child while he indulged in his hobbies. He tossed the cards onto a storage shelf and slipped his arms around her petite frame, cradling her against his chest.

"Oh, Ben!"

He felt a sob shudder through her. "It's okay," he whispered against her temple, tightening his hold on her until their bodies were so close they nearly melded into one entity. God, she felt so right in his arms. The agony of it made him ache. And to think she'd been right under his nose while he'd been chalking up one disappointing date after another in hopes of finding someone who'd make him feel whole again.

He'd first met Laney three years ago when Scott and Josh ended up in the same grade-one class. She had a lot of sympathy for a withdrawn little boy who'd lost his mother the previous year. She'd earned Ben's eternal gratitude and friendship when she'd encouraged Josh to invite Scott to his birthday party. The boys had become fast friends soon afterward.

When Reese died, Ben had felt for her and Josh. He knew exactly what they were going through. He'd offered to help in any way possible...doing the odd repair job, cleaning out gutters, tossing baseballs and scrimmaging hockey with the boys.

He thought nothing of it when she'd offered to bake Scott a spaceship cake for his birthday party in August or that she'd sewn Scott's Superman costume for Halloween along with Josh's Spider-Man costume. Or that trips to the movies and museums often became foursomes. It wasn't until last November when Laney had asked him how long he'd continued to wear his wedding band after Rebecca passed away that he'd realized Laney had reached the point in the grieving process where she was ready to consider the possibility of a new relationship.

The more he contemplated the idea of Laney getting involved with other men, the less he liked it. He'd thought their friendship was the cause of his knee-jerk, big-brother overprotectiveness. But then Christmas arrived and it had suddenly hit him that he loved her. And because he loved her, he was going to be there for her, even though he wanted to strangle Reese Dobson with his bare hands. Ben pressed a light kiss onto her scented hair, kissing his dreams of a life with her goodbye.

Her sobs started to ease. "I'm s-sorry," she stammered, wiping her cheeks with the backs of her hands. "I didn't mean to fall apart on you."

"What are friends for?" he replied. The words penetrated his heart like a dull knife. "Listen, I understand why you want to go to Whistler. I'd move heaven and earth to see Rebecca again. But I'm not going to let you go alone. This sounds too dangerous.

I'm sure I can get my mom to watch the boys. What do you say?''

Her hands came to rest on his chest, on the damp spot her tears had made on his faded sweatshirt. Her clear blue eyes glistened with moisture, gratitude and trust as she tilted her head back and gazed up at him. ''I say you're the best friend I've ever had.''

Regret and desire formed a thick knot in Ben's throat. First and foremost, he and Laney would always be friends. ''Your safety and Josh's happiness are very important to me.''

She nodded, but a shadow appeared in her eyes that Ben didn't know how to interpret. She grasped a handful of his sweatshirt, catching a few of his chest hairs in the process. ''I'm going to pay for everything,'' she said brusquely.

Ben winced, more from wounded pride than discomfort. He covered her hands with his own and peeled her fingers away from his chest. ''We'll argue about that later.'' Even knowing Reese could be alive didn't diminish the rush of awareness Ben felt eddying through his veins at the joining of their hands. The scarlet blush rising in Laney's cheeks gave him the faint hope that she felt it, too.

''What'll we tell the boys and your mother? I don't want to get Josh's hopes up by telling him his dad is alive.''

''We'll tell my mother the truth and we'll tell the boys you and I are going away for a few days and let them draw their own conclusions. We can explain everything if we come back with Reese.''

Her mouth formed an *O* that could only stand for

a major objection. "You realize the boys will think we're dating or…*s-something*," she spluttered.

Laney just couldn't say it: *sleeping together.* It was too close to the most private thoughts she'd been entertaining about him in the last few months. She felt her face grow even hotter and dropped her gaze to Ben's broad chest. His paint-dotted sweatshirt looked as though it had shrunk to fit his muscular build.

Ben's strong fingers were locked around her own reassuringly. The symbolic iron professional engineer's ring he wore on his working hand gently scraped the tender flesh at the base of her fingers. An all-male grin flickered at the corners of his mouth. "I realize they'll think we're sleeping together. We can always tell them it didn't work out and we're still friends."

Laney bit her lower lip. That's exactly what she was afraid of. She knew Ben was offering a perfectly logical explanation for their being away together, but Scott was used to women coming and going in his father's life. Josh, on the other hand, might interpret their going away together as a sign of a commitment and start building impossible fantasies of Ben becoming his stepdad. Josh had suffered enough loss and disappointment in the last fourteen months.

"Laney, we'll worry about explanations to the boys after we know whether or not this valentine is a hoax, okay?"

She relented, hoping she was worrying about nothing. "Okay." If Reese was indeed alive, Josh would have his father back and she would have much bigger issues to deal with, such as how one went about picking up the pieces of a marriage after a fourteen-month separation. Like most couples, she and Reese had experienced their fair share of problems.

Ben let out a ragged sigh. "Now that we've got that settled, why don't you and Josh stay for dinner? Mom's making lasagna, there's plenty. Afterward, you and I can talk to her about taking care of the boys and make some plans. Good enough?"

Laney nodded. The prospect of flying out to the West Coast wasn't nearly as alarming, now that she knew Ben would be accompanying her. But she felt a twinge of guilt. Ben did so much for her and Josh already. Was he going to have to cancel a date for Valentine's Day or use up some of his vacation time because of her?

He let go of her hands. "Wait here a minute while I clean up my workshop. I've just got to throw something in the trash and I'll walk you upstairs."

"What are you doing in there anyway?" she asked, rising up on tiptoe to sneak a peek into his private domain. "Your mother and the boys are dying of curiosity." The smell of paint and sawdust tickled her nose.

"Nothin' any of you need to know," he replied gruffly, closing the door in her face.

Laney laughed and wrapped her arms around herself, tempted to inform him that she'd probably learn what the secret was from Scott and Josh anyway. The man had two spies in his midst. Her gaze fell on the valentine and the greeting card that Ben had tossed onto the storage shelf and her smile died. This was a pretty big secret to keep hidden from two inquisitive boys, who'd already concluded the Tooth Fairy and the Easter Bunny didn't exist. They'd spent from Boxing Day to New Year's discussing the boot prints Santa had left in front of each of their fireplaces and comparing the handwriting on their Christmas gift tags.

Laney had a sinking feeling her ingenuity was about to be sorely tested.

"MOM, CAN WE HAVE DINNER at Scott's house more often?" Josh demanded as they trudged over the slippery sidewalk toward home. Ben had offered to drive them, but Laney had refused. They'd already taken up enough of his evening.

"Depends on whether or not we get invited," Laney murmured. "Are you trying to tell me you liked Georgina's lasagna better than mine, or that you liked being able to play video games with Scott after supper instead of doing your homework?"

Josh shrugged his shoulders, obviously smart enough to back away from a trick question when it was presented to him. Laney squeezed his mittened hand and suppressed a wave of anxiety about what life held in store for them in the coming week. "We still have homework to do," she reminded him. "What's four times twelve?"

"Forty-eight."

"Nine times seven?"

"Easy. Sixty-three."

Laney kept him plied with equations until they reached the driveway and the familiar lights of home. She paused in mid-stride, an eerie feeling prickling her scalp. Was it her imagination or were there more lights on than when she'd left? She hadn't been in Josh's bedroom all day, and yet the table lamp on his dresser cast a halo of light against the navy mini-blinds.

Oh, Lord, was someone in the house?

Reese?

Her heartbeat thundered in her ears like thousands of tiny hooves as emotions of fear, dread, anger and longing stormed deep in her breast. What should she do? Had she been so distracted by Reese's valentine she'd forgotten she'd turned on the lights?

She gripped Josh's hand tighter.

"What's the matter, Mom?" he asked.

"Honey," she said, dropping her tone to a whisper. "I don't mean to scare you, but I think someone might be in the house. Do me a favor and go next door to the Munks' house. Tell them what's going on, and wait for me."

Josh yanked sharply on her hand and peered up at her, his pale eyebrows butting together beneath the band of red and green ribbing of his navy toque. "Aren't you coming with me?"

Laney curled an arm protectively around his shoulders. "No, I'm just going to take a quick peek in the kitchen window before we call the police. Maybe I'm imagining all this. Now hurry."

Josh didn't budge an inch. "You're not going inside, are you?"

Laney struggled to keep her voice from telegraphing her rising panic. "Of course not! I'd never do that." If it hadn't been for the possibility that Reese could be in the house, she'd have already banged on the Munks' front door and demanded they call 911. She placed her hand on the middle of Josh's back and said firmly, "Go, speedy bullet."

Seconds ticked by with the excruciating slowness of snowflakes meandering down from the sky as she watched his snowsuited form struggle through the deep drifts blanketing the neighbors' lawn and dash up the front steps. Laney was sure the Munks were home. Both their cars were squeezed into their postage-stamp-size driveway and the downstairs lights were on.

Caution and anxiety slowed her steps as she approached the side entrance that she used to carry groceries into the house. Just around the corner was a picture window over the kitchen sink that gave her a view of the robins pulling worms from the lawn in the spring. The house had a fairly open layout with wide doorways. She should be able to see into her small dining room and living area through the window.

Her heart quaked at the possibility of seeing her husband ensconced in his favorite chair, his thick, fair hair barely visible over the pages of the Report on Business section of the *Globe and Mail.*

But foreboding settled in her bones and froze the anticipation awakening in her heart when she got a close-up view of the boot print on her kitchen door. The door hung slightly ajar, its jamb splintered from the frame.

Laney turned and ran.

Whoever awaited her inside was not her husband.

Chapter Two

Ben brought his minivan to a sliding stop on the ice-slick street in front of the Munks' house. The sight of the police car in Laney's driveway shredded his guts to ribbons. What would have happened tonight had he not invited Laney and Josh to stay for supper? He grabbed the keys from the ignition and bounded out of the van before the engine had finished shuddering. The Munks' front door opened and he could see Laney's petite form silhouetted by light.

"Ben, in here, quick," she called, her voice carrying unnaturally high in the crisp night air.

Relief that both she and Josh were unharmed flooded through him as he hurried up the salt-sprinkled front walk to join her. She closed the door behind him, shutting out the cold, and gave him a quick, tight hug that didn't nearly satisfy the need he felt to hold her. Her eyes mirrored all her questions and fears as she pulled away. Ben had a few questions of his own.... Laney had received the valentine today. The timing of the burglary was downright suspicious.

"Where are the police?" he asked her in a low tone as he bent over to unlace his winter boots.

"Searching the house. He told us to stay inside. I don't know yet if they found anyone. What'll we do if—"

"Ben!"

Before Ben knew what was happening, Josh did an end run around his mother and pitched himself at Ben.

"Boy, am I glad to see you. Where's Scott?"

Ben straightened just in time and braced one arm against the wall to keep from losing his balance as Josh caught his legs in a stranglehold. His free arm circled Josh reassuringly. "Scott's at home with his grandma. I hear you're having some excitement around here?"

"Yeah! The police are here and everything. Do you think they're gonna catch the bad guys who broke into our house?"

Ben glanced at Laney over Josh's head. "I don't know, sport. I hope so."

"Me, too. I made sure Mom didn't go in the house."

"He was very brave," Laney said with a strained smile that told Ben how afraid she'd been. "He followed my instructions to the letter and came over to ask the Munks to phone the police."

Ben tweaked the freckled tip of Josh's nose, noticing the boy still had a firm grip on his leg. "Good job. I'm proud of you."

Josh beamed up at him with wide blue eyes. "Am I a hero?"

"You are in my book, sport. Real heroes do brave things even when they're scared. And I'll bet it was a little scary to think somebody could be in your house.''

''Yeah, maybe.'' A flicker of worry crossed Josh's face. ''Do you think the burglar took my Super Nintendo?''

''I don't know. We'll see what the police say. But even if they did take your game, your mom has theft insurance. You'll get a new one.''

''Oh, cool. Maybe I can get the new Nintendo 64. Wait'll Scott finds out.'' Josh released Ben's leg and did an excited dance that looked like something between the moonwalk and hip-hop.

Ben hoped everything would be as simple as replacing some material items. How long would it take the police to search Laney's house?

He saw Mrs. Munk hovering at the entrance to the kitchen, observing them. She pointed in the direction of Laney's house and mouthed that the police were on their way over. Ben couldn't see Mr. Munk. Most likely, he was out on their rear balcony watching the action.

Mrs. Munk pulled a deck of cards off the top of the refrigerator. ''Hey, Josh, look what I found,'' she said, crowding the hallway further with her wide bulk. ''How 'bout we play a game of War to the finish?''

She'd already lured Josh into the kitchen by the time the patrol officer knocked on the door and asked Laney to come next door with him. He had the lean, hardened look of a cop who'd seen it all.

''Did you catch anyone?'' Ben demanded.

The officer jerked a thumb at him. ''Who are you? Her husband?''

"He's a friend," Laney explained, zipping up her coat. "Can he come, too, Constable?"

Ben threw the constable a look that suggested he'd have more than he could handle if he tried to stop him.

"Of course." The constable waited until they were outside before he told them he'd searched the house from top to bottom. "There was no one inside. Doesn't look like much was taken. I'd say they were in and out in a few minutes. They were probably watching the house—it happens a lot. They learn your schedule...what time you go out, how long you're gone. Usually they're after quick drug money."

"They? Was there more than one intruder?" Ben asked, keeping a protective grip on Laney's elbow as they crossed the icy driveway.

The constable shrugged and glanced down at a little black notebook he carried. "There's two different sets of footprints on the kitchen floor. Have a look around. We'll need you to make an itemized list of what's missing."

Laney nodded mutely, her eyes huge in her pale face. Ben clamped his jaw tightly in anger when he saw the single boot print on the kitchen door and realized how easily Laney and Josh's home had been violated. Hell, one kick. Ben listened carefully as the officer explained how the integrity of the lock could be strengthened by securing the latch plate to the jamb with longer screws. He'd make damn sure this didn't happen again.

Laney stared at her kitchen as if she'd never seen it before. It looked almost the same as when she'd left it hours ago. The walls were still a pale rose with a black-and-rose floral wallpaper border at ceiling level. The counters and shelves were still cluttered with her collection of teapots. The only difference was that her purse, which had been hanging on the coatrack near the door, now lay on the dirty black-and-white ceramic tile floor along with its contents—except for her wallet. One of the burglars had stepped on her favorite lipstick and broken its case. She could see a trail of carmine smudges leading toward the hallway, telling her everywhere the intruders had been. A numb rage cloaked her senses. Why had this happened now—the same day she'd received Reese's valentine?

Was the burglary a coincidence? Or were the two incidents somehow related?

Woodenly, she retrieved her purse and clutched it against her middle as she fumbled inside it for her wallet. Reese had bought her the purse in Italy on a business trip. Her purse was empty. It was a hollow victory knowing the thieves had netted thirty-five dollars and her credit cards.

She couldn't imagine Reese breaking into their home with an accomplice to steal from them. That didn't sound remotely like the man she'd married. But then, she'd never imagined the man she'd married would abandon her and their son for fourteen months. "My wallet's gone," she shakily informed the constable and Ben. She suddenly felt reluctant to venture any farther into the house. What other discoveries would she make?

Ben must have guessed her thoughts, because he

clasped her hand and pulled her toward the dining area. Laney could feel the warmth and strength of his firm fingers shoring her up, coaxing her to follow him. Before Reese had died she'd always been the strong one, capable of handling anything on her own. Was it fear making her so dependent on Ben now?

"I can't tell that anything's missing here," he said. "The living room looks okay, too. The TV's still there, and the piano."

Laney forced herself to open her eyes and look around. Ben was right. Everything looked in place. There were just those mocking lipstick marks on the polished pine floorboards and the area rugs.

Feeling braver, she led the way to the narrow stairs and followed the marks into Josh's room. Someone had gone through her son's dresser drawers. His Winnie-the-Pooh piggy bank was on his unmade bed—along with a penny the thief had missed. Laney picked up the penny and rubbed it between her thumb and index finger. "They took the money Josh was saving up for an aquarium, but everything else looks normal—" She broke off with a short laugh. "Normal. My life feels anything but normal right now."

Ben touched her cheek, tucking a strand of her hair behind her ear. The gentleness of his fingers made her want to lean her head into his hand.

"It's only money," he said with a lopsided grin that made her heart flip-flop.

Laney smiled at him, feeling her eyes water. "You're right." She squared her shoulders and gripped the penny tightly in her hand for good luck. "Two more rooms to go." An audible sigh of relief escaped her as she walked into her office. She gave her computer screen a pat, glad she wouldn't have to scramble to get a new system up and running, and decided she could overlook the mess someone had made emptying her desk drawers. Her office hadn't been all that tidy to begin with.

"Funny the computer's still there," Ben commented. "Looks like the constable was right and they were only after cash."

The burglars had rifled her mahogany bedroom dresser with the same efficiency. All her knickknacks, photos and perfume bottles had been swept clear off the dresser top, along with the lacy Battenberg runner. Had the thieves hoped she'd hidden hundred-dollar bills beneath the runner?

The only items of value she kept in her bedroom were the pieces of jewelry Reese had given her, and trinkets he'd collected during his travels. Worry formed an acidic lump in her stomach as Ben helped her pick through the sweaters and lacy lingerie that littered her floor, looking for her rosewood jewelry box. Neither of them could find it.

Hands on her hips, Laney gulped in dismay as the realization sunk in that that all her jewelry had been whisked away. She toed a pair of nylons peeking out from beneath her eyelet bed ruffle. A lucky penny obviously didn't buy much good luck anymore.

"My wedding band and engagement ring were in there," she said, feeling her chin wobble. She bit down hard on her lower lip to keep from crying. Her head ached from the disconnected thoughts crowding into her mind. What would Reese think if she showed up to meet him without her rings?

Ben's eyes held a mixture of compassion and something else she couldn't define. For some reason it seemed very important to her not to go to pieces in front of him again. She needed to be strong for herself. For Josh. "I suppose you're going to tell me it's only jewelry?"

"Nope. It's a symbol of Reese's love for you. Even though the symbol's been stolen, the love remains in your heart."

Laney glared at him. Spoken like a pragmatic engineer. The man had an answer for everything—except for why a man would stay away from his wife and son for over a year. There his wisdom had dried up. Laney knew it was because Ben was too kind to suggest the obvious possibility—that Reese had stayed away because he didn't love her anymore.

Had she nagged him too much about being away from home so often?

"Has anyone ever told you you're too practical?" she snapped.

Ben shoved his hands into the pockets of his jeans, his expression bleak. "Yes, lots of people. Many times."

Laney had the impression she'd hit a sensitive nerve and it sucked the anger from her. She'd never seen Ben look so vulnerable before. The dull gleam in his blue-black eyes suggested his thoughts were far from pleasant. Why was she blasting him, anyway? That damn valentine was responsible for seeding the bumper crop of doubts in her heart, not Ben.

All in all, Ben was right. She'd been lucky. "I'm sorry," she said, massaging her temples with her fingers. "I realize the burglary could have been a lot worse. I should be digging out my homeowner's insurance policy and the last appraisal on my jewelry instead of snapping at you for trying to make me feel better."

"Well, go dig them up," he said, brushing off her apology. "I'll meet you downstairs. I'm sure the police officer has other emergencies to tend to and Josh will be worried."

Her office files were still intact and Laney had no trouble finding the documents. But she took a moment to splash cold water on her face before she went downstairs. After the constable left, Laney straightened up Josh's bedroom. Then she went next door to get Josh while Ben rounded up some tools and scrap wood in the basement to effect a temporary repair on the door.

Laney brought Josh home by the front door, hoping to get him directly into bed, but her overexcited son made a beeline for Ben as soon as he had his boots off. Laney knew there was trouble ahead when he vociferously objected to the blocks of wood Ben had nailed up to secure the door for the night.

"It'll be fine," Ben patiently assured him, tapping a block with a hammer. "I used lots of nails. No one's coming through here."

Josh didn't look convinced. "But what if they come back after we're asleep? I wish Dad was here."

Laney's heart twisted with a pang as she put her hands on Josh's narrow shoulders and felt the tension stiffening his body. Was it her fault Reese wasn't here with them now? "We'll be fine, honey."

Ben squatted to Josh's eye level. "Josh, the burglars won't come back because they know the police will be watching the area. But if the door worries you, I'll be happy to stay the night on the couch—if it's okay with your mom. I'm gonna replace the door and the lock tomorrow and you'll be fine."

Laney's stomach quivered with alarm. Ben stay here all night? Her throat tightened convulsively at the thought of his rangy form sprawled on the floral sofa in her living room. Somehow it didn't seem appropriate to be wondering what her best friend wore or didn't wear to bed when she didn't even know if her husband was alive or dead. Where had that thought come from?

"Can Ben stay, Mom? Please?"

She closed her eyes, waffling. Josh would probably be up all night if she said no, and she had to report her credit cards stolen. But she didn't want him to jump to conclusions about the reason Ben would be allowed to stay over. "Sure, he can sleep on the couch. But only one night, until the door's fixed."

Josh let out a screech of delight that cleared out her ears. "Can we call Scott and have him sleep over, too?"

"No. Scott's probably been asleep for hours. Now, upstairs and into bed. You have school tomorrow."

"Aw, Mom."

Laney shooed him upstairs and prayed he'd obediently brush his teeth and put on his pajamas now that he knew Ben was nearby.

From the kitchen below she heard the occasional sound of hammering as she tucked Josh into bed and kissed him good-night.

"Where's Spidey?" he asked, yawning. He felt the bedclothes for the Spider-Man toy action figure he'd slept with every night since his dad had given it to him on his eighth birthday. "He's not here, Mom."

Laney checked the covers at the foot of the bed, then got down on her knees and looked under the bed. Why did things always go missing at the most inopportune times? She searched Josh's closet.

Josh's voice rose with fatigue. "Do you think the burglars took Spidey?"

"Of course not," she said, massaging a tight spot of tension in her neck as she surveyed the room. "It's probably downstairs by the TV. I'll tuck it in with you when I find it, okay?"

"Promise?"

Josh's plaintive wail melted her. She gave him another tight hug and a kiss, snuggling her face into the warm curve of his neck for a moment. The credit-card companies could wait. "I promise. Now go to sleep. It's very late." Then she turned out the light and escaped before he could sound another protest.

Her pulse fluttered at an accelerated rate as she jogged lightly down the stairs with a pile of blankets, sheets and pillows from the linen closet in her arms. Laney felt as if she were escaping one danger-laden zone for another. Ben was downstairs. He was spending the night under her roof.

"Josh get to sleep all right?" he asked with concern, joining her in the living room as she dumped her bundle on the couch. Laney had never been so aware of his presence before. The rugged maleness of him seemed so out of keeping with the feminine frills of her decor. There was nothing soft about Ben. His angles were hard and lean from his cheekbones to his shins.

"I'm keeping my fingers crossed," she said lightly, keeping her eyes averted from him as she scanned the floor area for Josh's toy. "Spidey's missing. Josh can't sleep without it, but I'm hoping he's too tired to put up much of a fuss." She looked under the cushion of a burgundy brocade Queen Anne wing chair Josh usually sat in when he played video games. "It should be around here somewhere."

"I'll help you look," Ben offered, opening the cabinet to the pickled pine entertainment center. He cleared his throat. "I hope you didn't mind my offering to stay over. Josh seemed kind of worried."

Laney risked a glance at him, noting the sleek darkness of the back of his head and the tempting span of his shoulders as he poked through the jumble of video and game cassettes. Guilt that she was even noticing how handsome and capable Ben Forbes was, trickled through her. Her hands trembled as she told herself that millions of married people made similar observations about members of the opposite sex every day. And it didn't mean a thing.

It was normal to experience the feelings from time to time, quite another to act on them. She would never do anything to jeopardize her friendship with Ben or the positive influence he had on Josh. Sometimes a child needed a man around, which was all the more

reason to find out if her son's father was still alive.
"No, Ben, I don't mind your staying over at all," she
said, grateful his back was to her.

Her reply sounded halfway convincing to her own
ears.

MORNING SO SOON? Laney's eyes opened wide at the
blare of the clock radio on her bedside table. She
rolled over to extinguish the sound and lay there, hoping Josh would be so absorbed with the idea of watching cartoons with Ben on a school morning that he
wouldn't notice Spidey wasn't in his bed when he
woke up.

They hadn't found it in the living room last night.
Ben had taken over the hunt while she'd reported her
stolen credit cards, but he'd come up empty. Laney
was feeling desperate enough that she planned to head
off to the nearest toy store to buy a replacement while
Josh was at school to prevent him from thinking his
favorite toy had been stolen. She'd rough it up a bit
so it wouldn't look brand-new.

Her gaze shifted to her dresser top, seeking out her
wedding photo. She was one day closer to finding out
whether her husband was alive. If he was alive, would
they ever be as happy as they'd been on their wedding
day?

Laney pushed herself up onto her elbows and
frowned. Something wasn't right. Where was her
wedding portrait? She'd cleaned up her room last
night, distractedly setting things up on her dresser
without consciously rearranging them, in hopes of
finding Spidey and... A current of alarm jangled

along her nerve endings as she realized she hadn't
seen the ornate pewter frame that usually sat on the
left end of her dresser. Laney wasn't a criminology
expert, but what kind of burglars had a taste for toys
and picture frames?

THE CALL CAME as he was watching a cruise ship slip
beneath the graceful span of the Lions Gate Bridge
from his West Vancouver penthouse apartment. Ivan
and Rico had been gone for two days. Plenty of time
to complete the job. They were professionals.

"What have you got, Rico?"

A low guffaw came over the phone line. "It's him
all right. We got a photo of the nuptials and the wedding ring he gave his bride."

"Excellent."

"We found a little bargaining chip, too. We'll have
him right where we want him. We'll teach him not
to screw with you."

"Were you careful?"

"Yes. She won't suspect a thing."

The man hung up with a smile. The hunting ex-
pedition had been well worth the expense.

Chapter Three

Laney glanced anxiously at Ben as the plane taxied down the runway with gathering speed, taking her toward her past and her future. Her stomach had contorted into a massive knot. She couldn't eat supper last night and she'd barely got three sips of coffee down this morning. Tomorrow, she was supposed to meet her husband—and she was petrified.

The lie they'd told Josh and Scott—that she and Ben were attending separate conferences in Vancouver wasn't sitting well with her either. Josh hadn't bought it...even when she'd told him Ben would probably be returning earlier than she. Thank heavens they'd opted to leave their skis at home, deciding they could rent what they needed to meet Reese at the appointed location. Skis most certainly would have aroused the boys' suspicions and, perhaps, have even alarmed Josh.

At least she wasn't worried about leaving Josh in Georgina's care. Josh was so excited about staying at Scott's house he hadn't even noticed the substitute Spidey Laney had purchased wasn't his original toy.

Ben's eyes were caring beneath the dark line of his

brows. A smile touched his clean-shaven face. "It's okay. I'm going to be right there with you," he said reassuringly.

Laney couldn't tell him that was the problem in a nutshell; not when he was being so generous to her. She realized now how unwise it would have been to go off alone. Yet, she felt awkward discussing Josh's attachment to Ben. "I know, it's just…well, you saw the boys' faces when we left. They know something's going on. Josh asked me last night if we were eloping."

Laney jerked her gaze away from the astonishment glinting in Ben's eyes and gritted her teeth as the plane took off, her face burning with embarrassment. This is just what she'd hoped to avoid. What if Ben assumed Josh's expectations were a reflection of her feelings for him? He'd run in the opposite direction as fast as his lean, muscular legs could carry him if he knew the tangy spice of the aftershave he was wearing this morning made her giddy.

Laney had heard the gossip during the hockey games. Whenever things started looking serious with a woman he was dating, Ben backed away. She was certain it was the fact she was off-limits that made their friendship work.

Ben quirked an eyebrow, his expression now carefully neutral. "What'd you tell him?"

Laney lowered her gaze to his jean-covered thighs, grateful there was no one in the third seat in their row to overhear their exchange. "The same thing you told Scott—that this was a business trip and it was a co-incidence the conferences were held at the same time.

I explained Vancouver is a popular conference site because winter is milder on the west coast. And, I emphasized that we're *just* friends.'' Laney frowned, hoping Ben's story was consistent with hers. ''Did Scott say anything to you?''

''He only asked why he and Josh couldn't come with us. I told him they couldn't miss school and that we weren't even staying in the same hotel.''

Which was another lie. They were staying in a suite with separate sleeping quarters. Ben had thought it was a wise precautionary measure. He'd even made the reservations at the Chateau Whistler in his name. They could ski out the door of the hotel to a lift that would take them to the Rendezvous, a lodge located halfway up Blackcomb Mountain. The resort's tourist information center had informed them that Christine's was a fine-dining restaurant with breathtaking views of the Whistler valley and was located in the Rendezvous.

She picked at a thread of her cable-knit sweater. ''I'm still nervous about this meeting. I don't understand why Reese would pick a place on a mountain. He knows I haven't skied since before Josh was born.''

Ben suspected Reese had picked the location because he could ski away and disappear if he spotted trouble, but he didn't know what good could be gained by sharing that with Laney. She was wound tight enough as it was. Of course the boys suspected something was up. Ben had never seen Laney so pale or withdrawn. He could detect hollows in her cheeks that hadn't been there a week ago. The customary liveliness glimmering in her blue eyes was noticeably absent.

"I don't like it, either," he remarked, exercising restraint.

Beside him, Laney sighed, a short wistful sound. "He probably thought it would be romantic and selected it because of the name."

Ben felt a force of anger throb from his shoulders to the soles of his winter boots and repressed a strong desire to kick the seat in front of him. He'd put his heart and soul into the valentine puzzle he'd made for her. He hadn't written a poem since high-school English, but the words had come easily because it was for her. Now his efforts seemed hokey and amateurish compared to the intrigue and drama of Reese's invitation.

Ben scowled, his ego still smarting from the way she'd downplayed the possibility that they could ever be more than friends a few minutes ago. *Face it, Forbes, you're playing out of your league,* he told himself.

No longer in the mood for conversation, he picked up the newspaper and tried to lose himself in a story in the business section about a ring of thieves robbing companies of their computer systems and selling the information to foreign countries.

All he knew is that Reese Dobson had better have a damn good explanation for what he'd put his family through.

LANEY SILENTLY WATCHED the skiers in multicolored ski suits gliding and cutting turns along the groomed runs that wove like wide white ribbons through the majestic fir forests of Blackcomb and Whistler mountains. Was one of them Reese getting in a last run before their lunch date?

Her stomach lurched, her thighs trembling with nervousness as the quad chairlift ascended the mountain at a breakneck speed. Beside her, three teenaged boys enthusiastically swapped stories about the powder, steeps and gates. It sounded like a foreign language to Laney.

Ben was in the chair behind her. They'd decided to split up when they got off the Wizard Express lift and joined the lineup for the Solar Coaster Express to take them farther up the mountain, so it would look as though she'd arrived alone. It couldn't have been a more gorgeous day.

Her goggles cut the glare of the sun beaming off the glistening snow. The ridges of the glacier-topped Coast Mountains were awesome against the backdrop of a pristine blue sky. Somehow it had seemed fitting that this was Reese's final resting place. He'd loved the mountains and the majesty and the thrill of backcountry alpine skiing. The steeper the better. He'd always been a risk taker. Was that why he'd wanted to meet her here—to show her he'd conquered the mountain?

The quad chair arrived at the top. Laney disembarked, gliding to a rusty stop on her skis. Adjusting her goggles, she filled her lungs with a fortifying breath of moist air and shoved off toward the Rendezvous, aware that Ben would remain close within her range. She owed him a big thank-you when this was over.

Nerves made her clumsy as she locked up her rental skis and walked toward the entrance to the large, flat-roofed, gray lodge. She removed her goggles and toque as she climbed the metal grate steps and quickly smoothed her hair, swiveling her head left and right in an effort to spot Reese. The place was packed. A large crowd gathered around the information desk. The din of voices from the Mountain Grill cafeteria was almost deafening. She found Christine's at the end of the building. It was quieter, more refined, with linen-draped tables and silverware. The spectacular 180° view seemed to inspire hushed tones.

There was no sign of Reese at the tables within her line of vision. Laney struggled to find her voice as she asked if there was a reservation for Dobson.

"Right this way," the hostess told her with a smile.

Laney's heart pounded like an erratic rhythm on a bongo drum as she followed the hostess. Her eyes darted from table to table. Lord, where was he? The hostess stopped beside a table with a reserved sign. Red rose petals were sprinkled over the snowy-white cloth, just as their sheets had been sprinkled with rose petals on their wedding night. Laney's eyes welled with tears. Did this mean Reese wanted their marriage back?

Did she?

In the center of the table was an enormous bouquet of red roses wrapped in green paper and tied with a red velvet ribbon. An envelope addressed, "To La-

ney, With Love'' was propped against the fragrant
blooms. She didn't recognize the handwriting.

''This is your table,'' the hostess said. ''Your party
isn't here yet, but he should be soon. You're a few
minutes early. Have a Happy Valentine's Day.''

Laney murmured a numb thank-you and unzipped
her jacket. She draped it on the back of the chair that
faced the entrance and sat down so she could see
Reese the moment he arrived. Somehow she felt she'd
know in that first look whether things could ever be
the same between them again.

The couple at the table across from her were holding hands and seemed so much in love it physically
hurt to look at them. Laney worried her lower lip.
Glancing back toward the entrance, she saw Ben had
just come in. She gave a faint shake of her head to
signal that Reese hadn't shown up yet, and turned her
attention to the flowers. Their intoxicating perfume
told her this wasn't a dream.

She couldn't put off reading the card any longer.
Steeling herself, she removed it from the envelope
with clumsy fingers.

Happy Valentine's Day, darling.
Love,

                                                R.

The writing was not Reese's. Had he phoned the
delivery in to a florist?

Unconsciously tapping the card on the tablecloth,
Laney sat back to wait and debated whether she

wanted her marriage back. Of course she did. Didn't she?

Ten minutes later she was still alone at the table, toying with her silverware. She ordered a glass of white wine to steady her nerves.

As the minutes ticked steadily by and diners filed in and out of the restaurant, the realization that she'd been stood up solidified into stone in her stomach. At 1:45, she told the waiter she was going to the ladies' room and would be right back. The tears started to fall before she had the door to the stall closed, granting her some privacy. Laney muffled a sob with her hands. Why hadn't he shown up?

"Um, excuse me," a woman said, tapping on the door to Laney's stall.

Laney grappled with the roll of toilet paper so she could wipe her face. "I'm not finished yet." Just her luck. There were probably fifty other stalls in the utilitarian bathroom and someone had to pick hers.

"Is your name Laney?"

"Yes?" She reluctantly opened the door. Had Ben sent someone in after her to make sure she was okay?

A pretty woman in her early twenties with a mass of dark ringlets and a friendly smile beamed at her. "A man paid me one hundred dollars to give you a message."

Laney knew only one man who'd hand over a hundred-dollar gratuity without blinking: Reese. Anticipation snared her breath in her lungs. "Wh-what's the message?"

"I think you have an admirer." The young woman glanced down at her palm. Laney noticed an address written on it in ballpoint ink. ''The man said if you're interested, to meet him tonight around seven...but your boyfriend's not invited. This is the address: 24 Horstman Lane. Okay?''

Laney blinked in weak relief, feeling an enormous lightening of the leaden heaviness in her stomach. ''Thank you so much,'' she said, and repeated the address back to the woman. Reese must have been watching and noticed Ben. She flushed. Did he think she was involved with Ben? Or was he that paranoid about anyone but her seeing him?

Did it matter? Laney's chin shot up a notch. She hadn't done anything wrong. She was not the one who needed to apologize or make explanations. She was not the one who'd abandoned their marriage and their child.

But she'd come this far, and she wasn't going home until she'd seen Reese and knew the truth of what had happened. Someone had to stick up for Josh's rights. But how was she going to get to 24 Horstman Lane tonight without Ben's knowing about it?

BEN ALMOST CHOKED on his grilled vegetables when Laney sauntered over to his table after retrieving her ski jacket, her chin held high. He'd silently applauded the fact that she'd left the roses on the table.

''May I join you?'' she asked softly, her eyes suspiciously bright.

Compassion for her and outrage with her jerk of a husband warred in Ben's chest, yet he managed to keep both emotions in check so she could salvage her pride. He rose and pulled out a chair for her, careful not to give in to the urge to caress her shoulders. "I'd be honored if you joined me."

"I can't think of anyone else I'd rather have lunch with on Valentine's Day," she said tartly, sitting down. "You're the biggest sweetheart in the room."

Ben ground his teeth. Right now he felt like the biggest chump in the room. The woman of his dreams was saying all the words he wanted to hear, but it was all wrong. Her heart wasn't in it.

Laney ducked her head, her lashes concealing her eyes. "I'm sorry I led you on a wild-goose chase."

"I'm not. I've been thinking maybe my life is too dull." He gestured toward the view. "I mean, look at the world out there—it's beautiful. Scott and I have always spent my few weeks of holidays at the same campgrounds in Maine and Ontario every year. I should be taking Scott on a cross-country tour of Canada. We could camp along the way, make it a big adventure. Whistler has shown me I'm in a rut, so don't apologize."

Laney laughed, the old music almost back in her voice. A tinge of rosy apricot—that matched her turtleneck—crept into her cheeks. Ben had to mentally order himself not to act like an idiot by telling her that he would never stand her up. Never let her doubt that he loved her.

"Oh, Ben, you're not in a rut. I like you just the way you are."

She did? Ben's stared at her for a minute and saw the pain and determination in her eyes. Laney was one hell of a woman and maybe there was hope for the two of them yet. But first, he had to convince her to show the notes to the police and let them figure out whether or not Reese was still alive. Getting involved with a married woman wasn't okay in Ben's personal code of ethics.

She helped herself to a julienned carrot from his plate. "I'm starving. Let me have something to eat and we can spend the afternoon on the slopes. They must have some beginner trails for a rookie like me."

"You don't want to see if we can track down Reese?" Ben asked incredulous.

"No," she said with a resolute edge to her tone. "I've gone to all the effort and expense I care to. As far as I'm concerned—and until the law tells me otherwise—my husband is dead."

"I don't think it's that simple—" Ben broke off as the waiter appeared at their table holding the bouquet of roses. Laney told him to put them in a vase and let the other guests enjoy them. After she'd ordered an Italian flatbread sandwich and salad, Ben excused himself for a few minutes.

He caught up with the waiter near the entrance to the kitchen and appropriated the card that had come with the flowers. The florist's name was stamped on the corner of the envelope. "My friend is a little worried about her date," he explained. "Would it be possible to find out when the reservation was made and if there's a contact phone number?"

The waiter shrugged. "Sure, you can ask at the front. I hope her date didn't get lost on the mountain. He's probably stuck in lift lines."

Ben passed the waiter a twenty and hurried to the entrance to speak to the hostess. She told him the reservation had been made a week ago, but there was no contact number.

Ben refused to be discouraged. He could at least try the florist's shop. He zipped the envelope into the pocket of his ski pants and headed back to the table before Laney began to wonder what was keeping him. Laney might be ready to give up on finding Reese, but he wasn't.

BEN HEARD THE SHOWER in Laney's bathroom and scrawled a note on a pad by the telephone that he was going out for a few minutes to buy a newspaper. The florist probably closed at five on Sundays. He had to go now or he'd miss his chance.

Checking to make sure he had his room key, he grabbed his ski jacket and took the elevator down to the rustic stone-tiled lobby where he asked a bellboy for directions to the florist shop.

The cold air bathed his cheeks as his boots crunched in the snow dusting the cobblestone streets. Night had already descended on the valley. The temperature here was mild compared to Ottawa in mid-February. The alpine village was aglow with lights, the architecture of the cozy bistros, specialty shops and galleries reminiscent of a more European setting.

Ben found the florist with no problem. The sickly-sweet scent of flowers and potpourri bombarded his nostrils as he entered the shop. Six men were lined up at the counter ahead of him. The female clerk acknowledged him with a bemused expression as she wrapped a bouquet of carnations in heart-dotted cellophane. ''Just remembering it's Valentine's Day, eh?'' she said. ''There are still a few arranged bouquets in the refrigerator if you're in a hurry. But I warn you, there isn't a rose left in the valley.''

He flushed and decided to wait his turn, fiddling with the envelope in his pocket as he tried to figure out what to say.

''What can I do for you?'' the clerk asked, when it was finally his turn. It was past closing time, but the woman hadn't put the sign up on the door. Three other men had entered since he'd arrived, wallets in hand and desperate expressions on their faces.

''I was wondering if you could tell me who sent some flowers?'' he began awkwardly.

''Do you have a secret admirer?'' the woman asked, tucking a pen behind her ear. Ben noticed the bubblegum-pink sweatshirt she wore bore the slogan, Express Your Love With Flowers.

''No, I hope not. I wanted to know who sent a dozen roses to Laney Dobson today at Christine's restaurant on Blackcomb.''

The clerk frowned. ''Wasn't there a card?''

''Yes, but—'' Ben pulled it out of his pocket.

Before he could stop her, the woman had opened the card and read it out loud. Ben winced. He hadn't wanted to invade Laney's privacy by knowing what Reese had written. At least the message was a tame Happy Valentine's Day wish.

''Oh, I see what your problem is,'' the clerk went on. ''You're wondering who *R* is?'' Her lively green eyes boldly skimmed over him. ''Frankly, I don't know what you're worried about, handsome, but I could look up the invoice for you to give you a little peace of mind.''

''You don't understand,'' Ben protested, reddening.

''Actually, I do. You don't know how many misunderstandings arise out of Valentine's Day flowers. Usually turns out it's a relative or a co-worker just being nice because they don't have anyone special in their lives. It makes them feel better to send flowers to someone.'' The woman flipped through a pile of invoices attached to a metal ring. ''Dobson, here it is. Ordered by Reese Dobson last Tuesday. Paid cash.''

''That's my wife's brother,'' Ben stuttered, finally giving in to the clerk's nonsense. ''Did he leave a contact number or something? When he's up here, he's usually bumming off friends and we really need to get ahold of him. There's a family emergency.''

''Sorry, there's no number or address because he paid cash,''

''Do you remember the order?'' Ben asked. ''Or anything he might have said to you?''

The clerk shook her head. ''We get so swamped this time of year, I can't remember one order from the next. I wish I could be of more help. Good luck finding him.''

Ben sighed and turned away. He'd have to find Reese some other way.

To his dismay, he realized he'd been gone almost an hour and a half by the time he got back to the hotel room with a newspaper tucked under his arm. He hoped Laney wouldn't be upset with him. When he realized the shower was still running, he relaxed.

She'd never even noticed he was gone. Then Ben straightened. He'd heard of women taking a long time in the bathroom, but this seemed a bit extreme.

He knocked on her bedroom door and called out her name. When there was no answer, he turned the knob. It was unlocked. Ben headed for her private bath and knocked on the door. "Laney? Are you okay in there?"

Fear gripped his heart at her lack of response. All he could hear was the sound of water drumming. He tried the knob. The door was unlocked.

He shielded his eyes as he opened it. The room was filled with steam, but the shower curtain was drawn. "Laney?" Ben pulled the curtain open. The shower was empty.

Laney had given him the slip while he was in the shower earlier. Where the hell was she?

IT TOOK ONLY SECONDS for Ben to conclude she'd probably gone to meet Reese on her own. He couldn't imagine Laney leaving the shower running just so she could slip out for a breath of fresh air, unless she was so shaken by Reese's not showing up that she was walking around in a daze.

Regardless, he had to find her.

A quick search of her room told him she'd taken her purse with her and probably the spare key to their rental car.

He wrote her a note that he was going out to look for her and asked her to stay put until he returned. Then he left the room. His heart jammed in his throat as he approached every bellhop in the lobby and described Laney. None of them remembered her. His luck improved with the concierge.

"Sure, I remember her," the perky blonde replied in answer to his questions. "She asked me how to get to Horstman Lane."

"She did? Can you tell me how to find it?"

The concierge laughed and pulled out a map of Whistler. "I'd be delighted. It's not far—easily within walking distance if you don't have a car." She circled a street.

Ben thanked her and took off at a run through the lobby, the map clenched in his fingers. The thought of Laney being alone with Reese worried him. What if she was walking into some kind of trap?

Laney hadn't taken the rental car. Ben found it in the parking lot and jammed the key into the ignition, figuring it would be faster than following her on foot. The engine roared to life, the wheels slipping on the ice as he backed out of his parking spot. He'd bang on the door of every single house on Horstman Lane until he found her.

WALKING AT NIGHT had never bothered Laney before, but walking under the stars was different than walking under a lamp-lit street. The trees here were so tall and solemn, their branches dark with secrets. An apprehensive chill clung to her neck like a clammy scarf as she peered at the massive chalets tucked back from the darkened street and tried to make out house numbers.

Had Reese been living in Whistler all this time? Her heart pounded loudly in her chest, echoing the sound of her footsteps breaking the crust of the snow covering the roadside. Twenty-two. The next house should be twenty-four. Her breath caught in her lungs at the sight of the modern wood-and-glass structure that loomed out of the hillside. It was three times bigger than her home. A black Mercedes was parked on the circular drive paved with gray interlocking brick. She could see the glow of candlelight through the windows on the lower story. The rest of the house looked dark.

With trepidation, Laney marched up the steps. She had to do this for Josh. The front door was spectacular and looked like a sheet of glacier ice. It was ajar a few inches. She peered through the crack then pushed it open. A path of white rose petals led off a luxurious Persian rug into the dark granite foyer. The source of the candlelight she couldn't determine.

''Reese? It's me,'' she said faintly.

He didn't answer. Anxiety, happiness and fear made her pulse throb at the base of her throat. Did he want her to enter? Obviously, so. He'd always been a crazy romantic. She felt guilty that Ben's presence had spoiled Reese's plans for their lunch.

Laney crossed her fingers for courage and stepped into the foyer. A stone staircase curved up to a second floor and she could see a faint light in the crack of the door. But the rose petals led in another direction. Laney shrugged out of her coat and kicked off her boots, then followed the rose petals to a pair of doors with the same crackled glass, through which she could see the cast of light.

A huge candelabra placed on a marble-topped side

table illuminated an elegant living and dining area decorated with sculptures and furniture pristine in their beauty. Gleaming silver domes rested over two place settings on the massive pale wood dining table. Three single candles flickered from crystal holders spaced along the center of the table. The appetizing odor of food lingered pleasantly in the air. Laney could see a bottle of champagne resting in a silver bucket of ice.

There was no sign of Reese, but she refused to believe she'd been stood up again. "Ben doesn't know I'm here," she said, raising her voice so Reese could hear her from wherever he was concealing himself. Laney followed the scattered petals around the grouping of cream leather sofas to the dining area. What did he want her to do? Sit down? Perhaps he meant to serve her as he'd done during many of their romantic interludes.

She ran her hand over the back of the chair. Was Reese in the kitchen, then? "Darling, please come out. I don't think I can stand the suspense a moment longer."

The house answered her with silence. Laney waited, anticipation screaming from her pores.

Still, nothing.

Setting her jaw, she ignored the rose petals and walked toward a door she believed must lead into the kitchen. It was almost six-thirty. Perhaps Reese hadn't expected her to arrive so soon.

The kitchen was dark, but she found the switch. The stainless-steel panels of the restaurant-quality appliances shimmered against the stark whiteness of the cupboards. There were cartons of Chinese food warming in the oven.

Laney turned on her heel. She'd seen a faint gleam of light upstairs. That's where Reese must be. If he wasn't, she'd leave. Her heart couldn't take any more of this. She didn't need drama and suspense in her life. She needed a man to hold on to at night. Every night.

The staircase was dark and she clung to the rail as she mounted, wishing she'd bothered to find a light switch for the chandelier over the stairwell that reminded her of a frozen waterfall of icicles. Light glowed through another pair of crackled glass doors at the head of the landing. Laney touched the glass and said a small prayer. Then she turned the chrome knob and stepped into the master suite and met her husband's gray-eyed stare.

Reese was leaning back into a mountain of snow-white pillows heaped on the bed.

The scarlet stain on his blue silk pajamas told her she was too late.

Chapter Four

The woman's scream pierced the stillness of the night and opened a vein of terror feeding directly to Ben's heart.

"Laney!" he bellowed, running down the dark street toward the sound, his arms and legs pumping. Damn it, this couldn't be happening. Which house? There were two here at this end—a large contemporary monstrosity shared the hillside with a cedar-log cabin. Ben pulled up short on the road, chest heaving, as the cold air burned in his lungs, and listened. Nothing.

The scream had stopped.

Ben couldn't even let himself speculate on what that could mean. He'd already lost one woman he loved. There were more lights on at the log cabin, but Ben made a split-second decision and chose the monstrosity for its sheer, clamoring pretentiousness. Fear swelled in his throat as he pounded up the steep brick drive and leapt onto the front step. The damn house looked eerie. Hell, what was that? Candlelight glowing through the door?

The melodic ripple of the doorbell made the skin

crawl at the back of his neck. He couldn't hear any footsteps. Ben banged on the door, then decided he couldn't wait for niceties and opened the damned thing himself. It would suit him just fine if someone called the police. The door opened easily on silent hinges. A woman's soft, broken sobs trickled down the stairwell into the cavernous foyer. He saw a pair of boots in a puddle of melted snow and Laney's ski jacket draped across a carved chair.

Ben's stomach clenched with dread. If Reese had hurt her, he'd...

Caution heightened his senses as he stole across the foyer and took the steps two at a time, mindful that the stone treads could well be taking him to something he didn't wish to see. A muted pool of light spilled onto the carpeted landing from an open door. Halfway up the staircase, Ben peered over the edge of the landing into the room and felt his knees turn to rubber. Laney was on the bed with a man, on her knees, leaning over him, her back to Ben. Ben didn't have to guess who the man was. Laney's near-hysteria told him it was Reese. Her shoulders shook as he heard her say between gulps, "I'm so sorry...."

Ben closed his eyes for a second as grief exploded like a grenade in his chest. *Reese was alive.* He should be happy for Laney. Happy for Josh. Ben thought about walking out of the house and finding his car, which he'd left near the head of the road when he'd started going door-to-door, but he couldn't leave Laney. Not yet. Not until he knew for certain Reese wasn't in some kind of trouble.

With a heavy heart, Ben mounted the rest of the

stairs and called her name from the doorway. "La-ney?"

She whirled toward him in fright, her eyes wild. Ben looked from the bloody towel in her hand to the glass rod embedded in Reese's chest. Ben's body turned ice-cold despite the heat generated from the gas fire blazing in the corner fireplace. Reese was in trouble all right, and now they all were.

Laney stared at Ben as if he were a ghost. She'd never needed anyone as much as she needed him right now.

"Oh God, Ben, help me! Call 911. Maybe they can still save him." Her hands trembled as she bunched the towel over the wound in Reese's chest and bent over to breathe more air into his lungs.

His skin was still warm, but she couldn't find a pulse. Vaguely, Laney heard Ben's anxious voice on the phone through the dense fog of fear enveloping her mind. Somehow she knew that no matter how many times she breathed air into Reese's lungs, he was irrevocably gone from her. Why hadn't she been more careful when she'd gone up the mountain this morning? Had he risked his life to come out of hiding to see her?

Laney straightened and felt the comforting brush of Ben's palm on her back as he joined her at the bed. "An ambulance and the police are on their way," he told her, his fingers searching for a pulse in Reese's neck. Her eyes met his and Laney knew the horror she was living was real because it was reflected back at her in Ben's eyes.

Reese was dead.

The police? Oh, God, what was she going to tell the police? "It's my fault," she told Ben, feeling the hot glide of tears wetting her cheeks.

"Wh-what do you mean it's your fault?" Ben said tightly.

She stroked Reese's face. His fair hair had thinned at the temples in the last year and he combed it differently. How could he seem so familiar and yet a stranger at the same time? Her jaw quivered with the effort of trying to contain the emotions pummeling her heart. They'd missed so much in the last year.... Her chest ached with the hollow ring of renewed loss. Why had it come to this? "I think he canceled lunch because he saw you. If I'd met him then, this might not have happened. Someone else must have found out about this meeting."

"Laney, it's not your fault. And if you had met him, maybe you'd be dead, too." Ben's bluntness was underscored by the wail of approaching sirens.

Laney turned to him, numb with shock at the prospect of Josh growing up without her. Could Ben be right? Someone had killed Reese. Were she and Josh in danger now? "Oh, Ben, what am I going to do?"

Ben's arms slipped around her and drew her into the safe haven of his chest. "Don't worry, it'll be okay. We'll get through this. Just tell the police everything you know...and for Pete's sake, don't tell them it's your fault."

"LET ME SEE if I have this straight, Mrs. Dobson," RCMP Corporal McBain said, incredulity sneaking into his tone. "Your husband died here at Whistler in an avalanche over a year ago. But somehow he survived and sent you a valentine with an invitation to meet him for lunch today—only he doesn't show up. Instead, a woman whom you meet in the ladies' room—whom you can't name—gives you an address and you show up, only to find your husband dead?''

"I know it sounds like the plot of a TV movie, but it's the truth," Laney said, glancing warily at the large-boned officer dressed in gray corduroys and a navy fisherman's sweater. McBain was a barrel of a man with a voice like a ringmaster that seemed to carry into the vaulted ceiling of the log cabin. She hoped Ben couldn't hear him. Ben was in another part of the house with a constable. Laney was so distraught, she and Ben had been taken to the house next door—the log cabin being the home of a friend of someone on the force. A forensics team from Vancouver had been called in to comb the house. A police dog had already been dispatched from Squamish and was conducting an outdoor perimeter search on the off chance Reese's assailant had dropped something. Laney clutched the mug of lemon-scented herb tea the homeowner had thoughtfully made for her. "I have the valentine and the other letter to prove it back in my hotel room," she insisted.

"We'll send someone back to your hotel with you to pick them up," McBain replied. "Does the name Graham Walker mean anything to you?"

She mulled it over for a minute, then slowly shook her head. The name didn't ring a bell. "Should it?"

Corporal McBain's expression was infuriatingly bland as he pronounced, "According to the ID we found in the victim's wallet, his name is Graham Walker.''

"Graham Walker?" Laney frowned. "I don't understand. Are you suggesting he wasn't my husband at all, but a look-alike? Why would someone pretend to be Reese?"

"I'm not suggesting that, Mrs. Dobson. But at this stage in a homicide investigation we don't rule out anything. How were your relations with your husband before his initial disappearance?"

"Fine." She stared down into her mug, not caring for this line of questioning any more than the last. "Reese was always a romantic man to be with."

"No arguments?"

"I wanted him to be home more—he traveled a lot with his work. But I wouldn't call our discussions about his schedule arguments."

"Do you have any children with the victim?"

"Yes. We have a nine-year-old son, Josh." Laney swallowed hard and felt a shudder rock through her. "He'll be heartbroken about his dad. He's—we've—missed him a lot. I can't think why he'd let us believe he was dead."

"We'll do our best to find out, ma'am. I realize this is a shock, but it is necessary for me to ask certain questions that may seem indelicate."

"I understand."

"What's your relationship with Mr. Forbes?"

Relationship? Laney blinked, not quite liking the way McBain rolled that word off his thick tongue. "We're friends—our sons are friends. He came along because he was worried about me meeting Reese alone.''

''Are you romantically involved?''

Laney resisted the impulse to glare at him. She could just imagine McBain putting two single parents together and coming up with one motive for murder. ''No. And I don't see what this has to do with who killed Reese—and why he disappeared.''

McBain shrugged his shoulders and made a note in his notebook. ''Let's go on to what happened this evening. What time did you leave the hotel?''

''Between five-fifteen and five-thirty.'' Laney sighed. She hated to think of Ben going through this same rigmarole in the other room…all because of her.

''CAN YOU THINK of any reason why Mrs. Dobson would want to kill her husband?''

''Why would she—when she could have ignored the notes and continued on with her life as if he were still dead?'' Ben asked. Frustration climbed his back like a cat digging in its claws. He closed his eyes and threaded his fingers through his hair, trying to dismiss the image of Laney on the bed beside Reese, the towel in her hands. Not for a moment did he think she'd killed Reese, but he wasn't sure what kind of conclusions the police would draw.

How had she known to meet Reese at the house? Why hadn't she told him about the meeting? The police had separated them before he had had a chance to ask her.

''She loved her husband very much, Constable,'' Ben said after a minute. ''She was overjoyed at the prospect he might still be alive. I honestly don't think she would have allowed me to come with her if she had had murder on her mind.''

''Yet you say she left the hotel without telling you where she was going. Didn't you find that odd?''

''Not if she was convinced that my being at the restaurant this afternoon was the reason Reese stood her up at lunch.''

''You don't know how she knew to find this address?''

''No. Your guess is as good as mine.'' Ben shifted in the overstuffed armchair in the library and studied the books clumped in untidy piles on the pine shelves, mostly murder mysteries, westerns and thrillers.

''Is she seeing anyone, Mr. Forbes?''

Ben glanced back at the young officer, who barely looked old enough to sport chest hairs. ''I don't think so. We don't usually discuss our social lives with each other, but sometimes her son says stuff that leads me to believe she isn't dating yet.'' Ben suddenly remembered his conversation with Laney in November when she'd solicited his opinion about removing her wedding rings. Had she been considering dating someone whom Josh hadn't known about? He pushed the disturbing thought away.

''You weren't dating her?''

Ben thanked his lucky stars he'd never officially asked Laney out on a date so he could answer the question with all honesty. ''Nope. We're friends. She was great to my little boy when my wife died and I've been trying to return the favor. What happens next, Constable?''

"Corporal McBain will have a few questions for you when he's finished interviewing Mrs. Dobson. Once the Ident team arrives, we'll want to take your fingerprints and Mrs. Dobson's fingerprints to help us identify your movements in the crime scene. Then, you're free to go. After we have the autopsy and forensic results, we'll know more. Of course, we'll ask you and Mrs. Dobson to keep us advised of your whereabouts as the homicide is being investigated."

Ben nodded, anxious to see how Laney was holding up.

As Corporal McBain strode into the library and conferred with Constable Henry, Ben mentally prepared himself for round two. Something about the big man's determined expression told him the police corporal had something particular on his mind.

"Mr. Forbes, how would you describe Mrs. Dobson's parenting abilities?" McBain began without preamble.

"She's a great mother, very kind and giving. Josh is the center of her universe."

"So she might react very strongly if she thought her son were about to be taken away from her?"

"That isn't what I said," Ben protested, feeling a state of alarm settle beneath his skin.

"You don't think her husband might have contacted her because he wanted to see his kid—maybe wanted custody?"

"Why would he send her love notes, then?" Ben asked.

"That's just it, Mr. Forbes. He didn't *send* them. She just claims she received them. Which would explain why the husband didn't show up at the restaurant. Mrs. Dobson claims a woman approached her in the ladies' room with a message from her husband asking her to meet him at the house next door.''

Ben's stomach reeled as he realized what Corporal McBain was driving at. "You think Laney set this up, don't you?"

McBain clapped his hand on Ben's shoulder. "It doesn't matter what I think. The physical evidence will tell us what really happened this evening. That you can bet on, Mr. Forbes.''

THE POLICE WEREN'T wasting any time gathering evidence.

A sick feeling continued to hover in Ben's stomach as he watched Laney hurry into her bedroom and return almost immediately with the note and the valentine, which she wordlessly handed to Constable Henry, who'd accompanied them to their hotel suite. Ben was sure the sharp-eyed young constable noticed the nervous twitching of her hands.

"Thank you, ma'am."

Laney closed the door after the constable took his leave and sagged against it, her blue eyes shimmering with confusion, pain and uncertainty. One look at her swept away the suspicions McBain had planted in Ben's heart. This was *his* Laney, whose expressive eyes were a constant mirror of her feelings. Vindictiveness wasn't part of her nature and never would be.

Ben was convinced the physical evidence would prove her innocent.

He took two steps across the room and gripped her cold hands. "You holding up okay?" he asked. "Come sit down and I'll pour you a drink. There must be some brandy in the bar."

"I could drink anything right about now," she admitted, allowing him to lead her to the sofa. "I feel so cold inside. A part of me keeps saying that it's impossible to lose your husband twice. What will I tell people? What will I tell Josh?"

Ben got her settled and gave her fingers a comforting squeeze. "You'll find the right words. Right now I'm more concerned about you and Josh than other people. I'm going to call my mom and make sure she doesn't let the boys out of her sight until the police know what happened to Reese."

Ben poured a brandy from the bar and carried it over to Laney. He was tempted to have one himself, but he didn't want anything dulling his wits right now. Laney stared off into space, her fingers cradling the heavy crystal tumbler. But he could sense her listening to his end of the conversation as he spoke to his mother. Ben kept the call brief and promised to phone again when they had more news.

"Are the boys all right?" Laney asked as he joined her on the sofa.

"Yes, Mom took them out for pizza for dinner. They're both asleep now. Mom sends you her condolences. She told me to tell you not to worry—she'll keep a close eye on Josh." Ben settled his arm around her shoulders and felt a lightening in his soul when she scooted closer to him and laid her auburn head against his chest. A shudder slowly wracked her body.

"Do you think it was Reese we found?" she asked so softly he had trouble hearing her.

He looked down at her. He could see the faint freckles—like Josh's—on the tip of her nose. "What do you mean?"

"Corporal McBain told me they found his wallet and the name on his ID and credit cards was Graham Walker. Didn't McBain tell you this?" She tilted her chin up to look at him with perfect trust in her eyes and Ben had to focus hard to keep from kissing her forehead and telling her exactly what McBain thought. That disillusionment could wait until tomorrow. Laney had had enough emotional shocks for one day.

"No, as a matter of fact, he didn't."

"Do you think someone was impersonating Reese?"

"Why would someone do that?" Ben cupped her head with his palm and felt the fine silk of her hair and the vulnerable softness of her cheek. "It's more likely he had fake ID. But I should think the police will be able to confirm his identity through finger-prints or dental records."

Laney gave a long, drawn-out sigh. "Which leads us to why he disappeared in the first place and why he decided to come out of hiding."

Ben curled his arm tighter around her. "The police should have some answers for us tomorrow and in the next few days. But that doesn't mean we can't for-mulate our own theories and do whatever we can to help the investigation. Now, tell me what happened in the ladies' room.... I want to know everything you can remember about the woman who approached you. For all we know, she set you up for Reese's murder.''

LANEY WASN'T SURE what kind of explanation she expected from the police, but the knowledge that Graham Walker was married and lived in West Vancouver, sapped her already low energy reserves and made her knees knock together beneath the table in the stark interview room of the Whistler Royal Canadian Mounted Police detachment.

She'd stayed up half the night with Ben, trying to blot out the memory of finding Reese's body from her mind. Talking helped, but when she'd finally gone to bed the tears had come again. By sunrise, she was more than ready for answers, but she just hadn't expected this one and all its implications.

"Married?" she asked weakly. She folded her hands together tightly on the imitation-wood tabletop and waited for Corporal McBain to tell her how her husband could possibly be married to two women at the same time. There must be some mistake. Maybe this Graham Walker really wasn't Reese, or there was some kind of explanation....

"About six months ago," McBain informed her, glancing at a file he'd opened on the table. "Interesting thing is he told his wife Kristel he had no family and he'd never been married. The house on Horstman Lane is their second home—purchased after their wedding. According to his wife, Graham left for Europe two days ago to meet with various clients. He owns a specialty wine importing and exporting company. He was supposed to be gone a week."

"But he obviously lied to his wife and didn't go," Ben interjected.

Laney winced inwardly at Ben's use of the word *wife* and tried to absorb the details of what McBain was saying.

"Apparently," McBain agreed.

"When will you have the autopsy results?" Ben asked.

"We'll receive some results later today. The autopsy is scheduled for this afternoon. Autopsies are conducted at the Vancouver General Hospital and the lab tests take a couple of days. In the meantime, we've already determined that Mr. Walker doesn't have a criminal record. We're running his fingerprints through Ottawa to see if there's a match, which will give us a positive ID on the body, but it'll be late tonight or tomorrow morning before we have those results."

"What if there's no match?" Laney murmured. "I don't think Reese ever had his fingerprints taken."

McBain cleared his throat. "That's a real possibility. Graham Walker might not have had his fingerprints taken either. If that's the case, we'll compare your husband's dental records with Graham Walker's records to see if they're the same person. Perhaps you could provide me with the name of your husband's dentist?"

Laney dug her dentist's business card out of her wallet and gave him the information. "Corporal, you said Graham and Kristel married six months ago. Do you have any idea when they met?"

"A few months before that. I believe they met at

a charity event on Grouse Mountain in North Vancouver."

"Well, don't you see," Laney said excitedly, "Reese could have suffered amnesia as a result of the avalanche and constructed a new life for himself. Maybe his memory came back, which led him to contact me."

"And maybe Graham's wife got suspicious and followed him to Whistler," Ben pointed out. His cheeks flushed. "Anyone who entered that house last night would assume a romantic tryst was taking place. Where was *she* last night, anyway?"

"She spent most of the day at home working on sketches for a project—she's an interior designer. She claims she spent the evening at home alone watching a video."

Ben's blue-black eyes narrowed. "Have you talked to anyone who can confirm that?"

McBain leveled his gaze on Ben. "You can be sure we'll be checking out her alibi and Graham Walker's background thoroughly. We'll be checking out yours, too. Neither of you mentioned you were sharing a hotel room. Maybe you were upset when you found out Mrs. Dobson was having a tryst with her husband."

Laney would have crawled under the table in embarrassment had it not been for the fact that McBain had no call to be singling out Ben. Even if they were having a hot, torrid affair, they wouldn't have been doing anything wrong. She opened her mouth to reply, but Ben beat her to it.

"We're sharing a suite—as in separate bedrooms,"

he coolly corrected McBain. "Since we didn't know what kind of situation Laney could be walking into, it seemed a wise precaution to take."

"Corporal," Laney said, endeavoring to change the subject away from her lack of an intimate relationship with Ben. "Would it be possible for you to arrange a meeting between Mrs. Walker and myself? Maybe, between the two of us, we can piece together Graham Walker's life. I'm sure she doesn't like the idea that she's been married to a bigamist any more than I do. I know my husband. And I'm not ready to accept that he would fake his own death and risk possible prosecution as a bigamist, not when he could have simply told me our marriage was over and have filed for divorce. There must be something more here... something serious enough that someone would want to kill him."

McBain seemed to consider her request for a moment. "Wait here. I'll call Mrs. Walker from another room."

As McBain left the room, Laney felt Ben's fingers settle over her hands, warm and strong.

"Good for you," he said, his eyes glowing with approval in a way that made a cloud of heat form in her stomach. "Stand up to him. They'll be looking for easy, simple answers and I don't think there's anything simple about this."

"That's an understatement. But I don't like the way McBain's dragging you into this." Laney wet her lips. "Maybe you should go home, Ben."

Ben's jaw hardened mulishly. "I'm not leaving

you, Laney. Not today. Not tomorrow. And certainly not because the police want to include me on their list of suspects. They can dig all they want. We have nothing to hide. So get used to the idea of having me around until we receive some answers, okay?''

Laney laughed, a dry, choking sound. She'd never seen him quite like this before, but she felt darn lucky to have him so solidly in her corner. Moisture filled her eyes as she squeezed out a response. ''Okay.''

By the time McBain returned, his boots clomping heavily on the floor, determination had settled in Laney's pores with renewed strength. Ben was right. The idea the police could suspect him—or her—of killing Reese was ridiculous. She had to push to keep them pursuing the truth. She gazed up at the corporal expectantly.

''I'm sorry, Mrs. Dobson, but Mrs. Walker refuses to meet with you.''

Laney arched her brows. ''Refuses?''

McBain shrugged his shoulders. ''Her words, not mine.''

''*No* is not an answer I'm prepared to accept at this moment, Corporal,'' she said with unwavering steel in her voice. ''Could you provide me with Graham and Kristel's address in West Vancouver? My son needs to know what happened to his father.''

Chapter Five

Laney held her breath as she sought out the house numbers on the series of gates and fences that separated the rest of the world from the exclusive waterfront homes lining Marine Drive. The narrow road wound along the coast through dense trees, whose verdant boughs guaranteed seclusion and private views of the Burrard Inlet and the Georgia Strait. According to the map, they were getting closer.

McBain wouldn't give her Kristel Walker's address, but he'd hinted that it was public knowledge and should be relatively simple for them to find it by asking around.

Laney and Ben hadn't quite known what the corporal meant until a front-desk clerk at their hotel told them Kristel Walker was a member of one of the province's wealthiest families. Everyone familiar with West Vancouver knew where she lived. Someone on the staff gave them directions and a description of the house.

There was no snow here. Purple kale, winter pansies and a few early crocuses brightened winterbare beds.

They drove through a village and Laney told Ben where to turn so they could reach the oceanfront lane where the Walkers lived. The lane was jammed with parked cars. A crowd of people hovered outside a pair of massive beige wrought-iron gates centered in a high stone wall. Laney saw TV news cameras. "Uh-oh, I think this must be it," she stammered as Ben veered around a parked vehicle jutting onto the roadway.

"I'll try to find a place to park," Ben replied, driving farther down the lane. They ended up parking on the next block near a cluster of apartment buildings. As they walked closer to the gates she could see two security guards standing inside the entrance to the grounds. The grounds were spectacular. A shaded velvet lawn studded with shrub beds and statuary made for a grand entrance to a buff-colored clapboard house with blue awnings capping the diamond-paned windows.

It gave Laney an odd feeling to think that Reese might have lived here with another woman. But she couldn't change the past. The most she could hope for was a way to understand it.

She threaded her way through the crowd of people and addressed one of the guards. "Excuse me. Would you tell Mrs. Walker that Laney Dobson is here to see her?"

"Sorry, ma'am," the guard said. "We've been given strict orders not to let anyone in the gate. The Walkers aren't receiving visitors today."

"I'm sure Mrs. Walker will see me if you'll pass on the message," Laney insisted.

"Sorry, ma'am, but until I hear otherwise, the Walkers are not to be disturbed. You can try again tomorrow," he suggested helpfully.

A reporter turned on Laney and stuck a microphone in her face. "Do you know the Walkers? Do you know the identity of the person who was found dead in their Whistler chalet? Do the police have any suspects?"

Laney stared at the reporter in dismay and realized the cameraman was rolling tape. The last thing she wanted was for her husband's possible bigamy to be front-page news. Another microphone suddenly appeared under her nose.

She felt a hand grip her arm. "No comment," Ben said firmly and dragged her out of the crowd.

"I guess jumping the fence is out of the question," she muttered.

Ben grinned. "At the moment. But I have another idea that won't get us arrested for trespassing. We need some help from people who know this area. I have a few contacts in the regional branch office. If my memory serves me correctly, one of them has a relative who writes the society column for the local paper. Judging from the size of that house, we're dealing with some major money."

"I'm game." Laney slid into the passenger seat. "If that doesn't work, we can try the library. Maybe there was a wedding announcement posted in the paper with some background information on the bride and groom. For all we know, Kristel Walker may be bending the truth a bit to keep the world from knowing she was married to a bigamist. Which may be precisely why she killed him.''

Early afternoon traffic crowded Marine Drive. It took them half an hour to drive past the ritzy West Vancouver shops of Ambleside and thread through the more mundane commercial district of North Vancouver to Lonsdale Quay with its classy promenade and distinctively nautical modern architecture.

Fortunately, they found Dale Hibbard in his office. Laney was grateful for Ben's judicious explanation that they were looking into the unexpected death of a friend in Whistler the night before. The partition walls separating the office space in the building offered limited privacy.

Dale nodded and scratched the gray whiskers studding his jaw. ''I'm sorry about your friend,'' he told them. ''It's actually my mother-in-law who writes the column, but she's a barracuda and I wouldn't recommend asking her anything unless you want the conversation—or her interpretation of the conversation—broadcast all over town. But I assume you're talking about the body found in the home owned by A. J. Butterfield's daughter. I heard about the murder on the radio this morning as I drove to work. The news report said the identity of the victim wouldn't be released until family members had been notified, but they hinted the victim may be a friend of the family, who was staying in the house. Apparently, a couple of rental cars were spotted on the scene.''

Laney was relieved Dale didn't press for more details. Evidently he didn't share his mother-in-law's passion for rumors.

Ben's brows stitched into a dark seam. "Butterfield, as in the Butterfield car dealership we passed on the way over here?" he asked.

"Yep. One of many Butterfield car dealerships. Except A. J. Butterfield died a few years ago and his son Nelson is running the show. I suspect everything you'd want to know about the Butterfield family will be all over tomorrow's paper, if it didn't make today's edition."

"Do you know where Nelson Butterfield lives?"

Dale laughed. "Everybody knows where he lives— on top of the British Properties." He pulled a pad of paper from his cluttered desk. "I'll draw you a map. You can't miss the house—it's a baroque mansion modeled after some famous house A.J. saw once on a trip to Rome. It's got the biggest fountain you've ever seen, smack-dab in front of it."

They thanked Dale for his help, and wove through the maze of partitions to the elevator.

"What do you think?" Laney asked Ben in the privacy of the elevator.

Ben pursed his lips and glanced down at the map. "I think things are growing more complex by the minute. Kristel may not want to talk to us, but I have a feeling her brother Nelson might be interested in what we have to say."

Laney tucked her hand in the crook of Ben's arm and felt buoyed by the thought that they were making some progress. "Let's not bother with the map just yet. Chances are we'll find security guards at his front gate, too. The car dealership is closer. I have a feeling someone there will be able to get a message through to Nelson Butterfield in a hurry.''

THE BEAMING SMILE on the dealership manager's face dimmed in wattage when Laney showed him the family photo in her wallet and told him precisely what she wanted of him.

''I think Mr. Butterfield will want to speak to us, don't you, Mr. Wong? I, for one, would like to know how my husband could possibly be married to his sister.'' Laney had never played hardball in her life, preferring a more genial approach to getting what she wanted—particularly when it came to dealing with the fragile egos of writers, professors and nine-year-olds—but she was catching on fast. And she hadn't even said *please*.

Of course, Ben's no-nonsense expression and the fact he loomed head and shoulders above the manager helped. Mr. Wong escorted them into his office and invited them to be seated.

Darting an uncertain glance at Laney and Ben, his stubby fingers reluctantly punched in a phone number. ''This is Sam Wong. My apologies for phoning at an inconvenient time, but it's urgent I speak with Mr. Butterfield.''

Laney noticed a damp sheen of perspiration appear on Mr. Wong's bald head as he waited for Mr. Butterfield to come to the phone.

''Nelson, it's Sam. I have someone in my office who insists on speaking with you.'' Mr. Wong's Adam's apple bobbed in his throat. ''I don't know how this is possible, but she showed me a picture and says she is also married to your sister Kristel's husband. She tells me she will go to the media with the story if you don't agree to meet with her.''

Mr. Wong's ebony eyes widened. ''Yes, sir. I will pass on the message.''

Laney leaned forward as Mr. Wong neatly hung up the phone.

''Mr. Butterfield will meet you here in twenty minutes. You are to enjoy the hospitality of my office in the meantime. May I offer you some coffee or a soft drink?''

Laney's stomach rumbled. She'd hadn't had an appetite for breakfast and her body was reminding her she needed fuel. ''Coffee, please. Cream, no sugar.''

''I'll take mine black,'' Ben said.

The manager nodded and left them alone. Feeling pleased with herself, Laney shifted in the comfortable leather-padded chair and glanced at Ben's handsome face. A shock of midnight hair fell onto his forehead. ''Well, that was easy,'' she said. ''Twenty minutes. I wasn't expecting him to drop everything to come see me that quickly.''

''No, but I wonder if he wasn't expecting to hear from you.'' Ben fingers stabbed at the hair drifting onto his brow. Tiny lines she'd never seen before fanned out from the corners of his eyes.

''What do you mean?'' Laney felt a dart of alarm nick her breastbone. Since she'd discovered Reese's body last night, her heartbeat seemed to have settled into a permanently erratic rhythm.

''Just that I think he was expecting you to contact

him. I'm pretty sure that's why McBain told you how we could get Kristel Walker's address. Think about it. Why would a police officer do that?''

He had a point. ''Why do I have the feeling you're not going to say it was because of my powers of persuasion?''

The slow grin that inched over Ben's face as his gaze raked her from her boots to the top of her head made Laney's toes curl in feminine awareness.

''As delightfully charming as those powers are,'' he remarked with obvious amusement, ''I think we've been set up. We've probably been followed since we left Whistler. Heck, Dale Hibbard is probably being questioned as we speak. Now, I may have been watching too many cop shows, but my gut instinct is screaming that Nelson Butterfield will show up wearing a wire.''

''Oh, my God! Should we leave—''

''Hey, don't panic.'' Ben reached out and brushed his knuckles over the back of her hand. Laney felt the effects of that stroke travel up her arm like a tiny current of electricity. It had definitely been too long since she'd been touched by a man. She couldn't remember her last romantic encounter with Reese. The niggling fear that he'd left because he'd fallen out of love with her hovered unanswered in her thoughts.

She tried to focus on the problem at hand.

''It doesn't matter if the police follow us. Let them,'' Ben continued evenly, making Laney wonder just what, if anything, fazed him. ''It'll just prove we're telling the truth. Leaving now would only make us look guilty.'' Apparently single parenthood, lost mittens and being the object of a police tail didn't hit any of his pressure points.

The door opened and a curvaceous blonde, wearing a black sweater and matching skirt, carried in a tray of coffee and chocolate-drizzled croissants. Laney noticed the young woman cast Ben a look of appreciative interest as she set the tray on the manager's desk, but Ben barely seemed aware of her presence except to thank her for the coffee. Laney decided that part of Ben's appeal was the fact he was totally unaware of the effect he had on women. Of the effect he had on her.

A gleam came into his blue-black eyes as he smiled at Laney over the rim of the foam cup as if she were the only woman in the world. His voice, of course, was ever practical and kept her feet solidly planted on the ground. "Besides, I'm more than a little curious to hear what Nelson Butterfield has to say."

"WHAT IS THIS ABOUT?" Nelson Butterfield demanded coldly as he strode into the office and closed the door firmly behind him. He struck Ben as the kind of man who always got what he wanted, ruthless and sharp. Scott and Josh would have taken one look at Butterfield's craggy features and his bristle-brush, military-style haircut and pronounced him "lean and mean." Ben noticed Butterfield didn't remove his camel overcoat, which suggested he didn't plan to stay long and might well be wearing a wire.

"I'm Laney Dobson. This is my friend Ben Forbes," Laney said with the grace of a duchess. "No doubt you've been in contact with the Whistler police, so there's no need to explain how we've come to be here. But I have every reason to believe your brother-in-law was my husband Reese, who disappeared fourteen months ago in an avalanche.'' Laney held out a family photo from her wallet to Butterfield. ''This is our family. We have a son, Josh. He's nine.''

Butterfield eyed the small photo as if it were a particularly disgusting object. Then, letting out a heavy sigh, he pinched it between his fingers and held it closer to the light from the window. His narrow brow furrowed. ''I admit there is a resemblance,'' he muttered.

''There's more than a resemblance,'' Laney insisted. ''I *know* that's my husband.''

Butterfield handed Laney back the photo, his mustard-brown eyes narrow with suspicion. ''Just what is it that you want from me? I find your sense of timing—how shall I say it?—extraordinary. First, you happen to find Graham's body. Now, poor Graham hasn't been dead twenty-four hours and you're seeking me out and making threats about the media. Maybe the police would be interested to know of your actions.''

Laney folded her arms across her chest as though aware the bright purple and yellow pansies knitted into her sweater might undermine her tough-as-nails stance. ''I apologize for the threat, but it was necessary. I'm not exactly keen about broadcasting my husband's apparent bigamy to the world and I'm sure your sister feels the same, which leads me to why I requested this meeting. I need your help, Mr. Butterfield.''

''My help? Is that a clever euphemism for a monetary inducement to ensure your silence?''

Ben rose to tell Butterfield exactly what he thought of his suggestion, but Laney gave his wrist a restraining tug, signaling she preferred to deal with the jerk herself.

Her chin jutted up and a shower of steel sparks glittered in her eyes. "No, Mr. Butterfield. I don't give a damn about your money, but I do give a damn about what my son thinks of his father. And what I'm going to have to tell him. I find it hard to believe Reese would walk away from us like that...I'd much prefer to believe he suffered some injury in the avalanche that affected his memory. Or was forced to flee someone or a situation that meant him great harm. If I could talk to your sister Kristel, maybe we could piece together what happened and try to figure out who would have a reason to kill him."

Laney approached Butterfield. Her frank expression made Ben's heart ache. Her doubts and fears and determination were mirrored in her eyes and the trembling of her lips. "But your sister refuses to see me. I understand she's suffered a terrible shock—that your family has been dealt a blow—but I need to talk to her and I'm hoping you can arrange it. This *can't* wait. Sooner or later the police will have to release a statement to the media. If your brother-in-law's picture ends up in the *Globe and Mail*, there are hundreds of people who may recognize him as Reese Dobson and we'll have a full-scale speculation scandal on our hands. I'd rather take offensive action and provide an explanation up front."

Butterfield was silent a moment and Ben saw the shell of hardness lift from his features. "I don't know if it's possible," the wealthy man said finally, rubbing his forehead. "She's devastated. She hasn't left her room since she heard the news. She's always been frail and sensitive.''

Laney nodded in understanding. Ben knew the sudden glimmer of tears glistening in her eyes were for Kristel's grief.

''I don't mean her any harm,'' Laney said softly.

''It doesn't matter. She won't like you,'' Nelson said bluntly.

A faint smile tweaked Laney's lips as she sniffed and tucked her hair behind her ears. ''I don't see why she would.''

''You've got a point there.'' Butterfield moved away from the door and shoved his hands into the pockets of his overcoat. ''You know, I never cared much for Graham. Kristel fell for him big-time, but I always thought he was too smooth. Slick. He's the last kind of guy I'd want on the showroom floor selling cars these days. Sincerity is what sells nowadays. And you, Mrs. Dobson, have sincerity written all over you. I'll talk to Kristel. But she'll have questions. You said your husband disappeared when?''

Laney told Butterfield the exact date.

Ben eased himself into the conversation. ''Do you have any idea why someone would want to kill Graham?''

Butterfield shook his head. ''I honestly don't. We got along all right and he seemed to blend in well with our circle of friends. Graham was in importing and exporting specialty wines, but he traveled to meet with his clients so I've never met any of them. He didn't invite any of them to the wedding, but it was a small ceremony—only a few guests. His business partner Dallyn Vohringer was there, however.''

"My husband was a financial analyst," Laney said. "He's always appreciated fine wines. He kept our wine cellar stocked with finds from his business travels."

Ben cleared his throat. "Any hint there was trouble in the business between Graham and his partner?"

"Not that I'm aware of. The company's proven to be very successful. Kristel told me I could stop worrying that Graham had married her for her money."

Ben had no doubt Reese was accomplished at making money hand over fist. "Would you mind if I asked what date they were married? The police told us it was about six months ago."

Butterfield flicked him a cautious glance. "July tenth."

"Do you know when they met? That would give us some indication if Laney's amnesia theory holds any water."

"I think it was in March, but I wouldn't swear to it in court. She brought him to Easter dinner at our place, but I think they'd just been on a few dates. That's not exactly the information one confides to an overprotective older brother. You might try talking to Dallyn. I'll give you his phone number and address."

He consulted with an electronic notebook he pulled from the inside breast pocket of his overcoat. Extracting a business card from another pocket, he picked up a pen from the desk and wrote down the address for them. He handed the card to Laney. "Maybe this will help find answers for your son. Give me a call at five at the cellular number listed on my card and I'll let you know if I've had any luck in persuading Kristel to see you.''

"Thank you, Mr. Butterfield," Laney said, examining the card.

"Call me Nelson. We'll probably all be better acquainted before this is through and the police arrest Graham's killer. I hope to God they discover an explanation for this mess soon."

Laney nodded. "Whatever the explanation is—the only way we'll find it is by working together."

Ben gathered up their coats. They had a Vancouver city map in the rental car. Dallyn Vohringer was about to have unexpected visitors.

Chapter Six

Connoisseur Specialty Wines' offices in the West End, overlooking English Bay, were impressive. A glass door etched with clusters of grapes opened into a reception area boasting a rich wine-red carpet, a tasting bar and a stunning display case of the company's products.

With his business acumen and knowledge of the world markets, Laney could picture Reese doing well in this business.

As the receptionist buzzed Dallyn Vohringer, Laney stared at the realistic grape-laden trellis that formed the frame of the display case, her thoughts splintering in six different directions at once.

The croissants and aspirin she'd eaten in the car on the way over were taking the edge off a headache that had started as a result of missing lunch on top of a miserable night without sleep.

Dallyn Vohringer was effeminate in appearance with delicate birdlike bones in his face, shoulders and wrists. He wore his icy-blond hair slicked straight back on his head and looked as if he could have posed for an ad for the designer suit that hung loosely on his body.

He took Laney's hand and held it for a minute as she introduced herself. His fingers were cool. "Of course, I know who you are. But please, why don't you step into my office where we can speak privately?"

With a glance at the receptionist, he led them into a short corridor that branched left and right. Dallyn turned to the right. His cherry-paneled office had a commanding view of the water. The dim outline of Vancouver Island was visible on the horizon. He closed the door behind them and invited them to be seated. "My receptionist doesn't know about Graham yet," he said, sotto voce. "The police thought it would be better if we gave the impression he was still in Europe for the time being."

Laney exchanged a glance with Ben, who raised his eyebrows at this news. Dallyn sat down behind an antique desk.

"I'm sorry, Mr. Vohringer, this is a little awkward. I—I'm not quite sure how to begin," she stammered, feeling the heat of a blush seep into her cheeks. The fact that Mr. Vohringer might know more about Reese than she did was intimidating.

"It's quite all right, Mrs. Dobson. I confess I'm feeling the awkwardness of the situation myself. Graham never mentioned he was divorced."

Laney felt her face grow even hotter. She didn't even dare look at Ben. It was too humiliating. "Probably because we were never divorced, Mr. Vohringer."

"Oh." She saw the understanding dawn slowly in his dark eyes. "I see."

"We have a son, as well. Did Reese, I mean Graham, ever mention us?"

"No, I'm afraid he didn't."

Laney swallowed hard, not certain whether this was good or bad. But maybe if Reese had been recovering his memory he hadn't wanted to tell anyone until he had spoken to her first.

"I'm very sorry," Dallyn said cautiously. "I don't know why anyone would want to kill him. He didn't have any enemies that I knew of. Oh, there was a bit of friction with his brother-in-law, but I imagine that was par for the course with Nelson Butterfield. All that money tends to get in the way."

"What about his relationship with Kristel?" Ben asked.

Dallyn glanced from Ben to Laney as though reluctant to discuss the topic. "If you don't mind my saying so, they seemed very happy together. Quite a few common interests."

Laney bit her lip. "The police told us they were married in July and met a few months before that. Can you confirm when they met? I have this theory that Reese suffered amnesia as a result of being trapped in the avalanche and may have taken on another identity."

"Hmm. You know, I think there may be something to your amnesia theory. Graham never talked much about his family or his background. As for when he met Kristel, I can't say precisely. I've known Graham a little over a year. We met at a wine-tasting event before Christmas and we hit it off. Graham had inherited some money from a grandmother and was looking for a business to invest in. We came up with the idea of importing and exporting specialty wines and opened our doors two months later. In fact, we just celebrated a year in business last week. But now that I think on it, I seem to recall Graham giving Kristel a tour of the office in late April or early May. He was quite nervous so I had the feeling she must be someone special.''

Special. The word sank slowly into Laney's consciousness, needling her heart with yet another prick of pain. Were she and Josh not special enough?

Of course they were, she told herself sharply. Reese *had* remembered them, which is why he'd sent for her. So why, then, did the needling sensation not go away? Was there something here she wasn't quite seeing?

Beside her, Ben leaned forward, his hands braced on his knees. "What will you do now that your partner is dead?" His point-blank directness almost made her smile. Leave it to Ben to always be thinking of the practicalities and not get hung up on emotions.

Dallyn made a small sound. "Actually, Graham was more of an investor than a partner. He put up the seed money for the company and took on a cameo role in its day-to-day operations, but he certainly didn't run the company. And it's registered in my name." He lifted his hand and gestured at the walls. "This was his hobby—something he played at between rounds of golf and ski trips. A few weeks ago he told me he wanted to go to Europe to visit some of our clients, though I suspected his real destination would be the French Alps. Probably Chamonix. But to answer your question, I will certainly continue to repay the loan to Kristel. However, it's really too soon to be thinking of things like that,'' he told Ben reproachfully.

A stray thought made Laney sit up straighter in her chair. Reese usually liked to play a round of golf with a buddy. Maybe Graham had made other close friends since the avalanche and had confided in them?

"Did you attend Graham and Kristel's wedding?" Laney asked, hoping she could coax a guest list out of him—or at least a few names.

"Of course. We provided the wines."

"Do you remember the names of Graham's friends who were there? Maybe one of them could help us."

"I'm afraid I wasn't paying much attention," Vohringer said. "I'd brought a date and, with all the wine, I was comatose by the time the evening was over." The phone rang and Dallyn reached for it. "Excuse me," he told them, covering the receiver with his hand. "It's an overseas call."

Dallyn looked something up on the computer screen, then told the customer he'd have to check the warehouse for the inquiry because they were in the midst of updating their inventory. He promised to fax a price as soon as possible. Laney glanced at her watch. It was ten after four. Was Nelson having any luck convincing Kristel to talk to them?

Dallyn seemed almost uncomfortable as he tried to assure the customer he'd be in touch shortly. Sensing they'd taken enough of his time, Laney gestured to

Ben that they should leave. Mouthing a thank-you to Dallyn from the door, they slipped out into the hall, quietly closing the door behind them.

The gleam of a brass nameplate on the burgundy paneled door at the opposite end of the hall made Laney pause. Was that Graham's office? Instead of turning into the reception area, Laney nudged Ben and held a finger to her lips. Casting a furtive glance at the receptionist, who was humming at her desk, she signaled her intent to tiptoe down to Graham's office. Ben nodded and followed her. Maybe they could find something there that could help them.

The door thankfully, was not locked. Laney felt her feet mire in the luxurious carpeting as she gazed at the room. The decor bore touches of Reese's personality. The rich leather wing chairs. The Marlborough legs on the English mahogany desk, the art showcased on the handsome cherry shelves. A photo on the desk in a brass frame caught her instant attention. Her heart hammering wildly in her chest, Laney ordered her feet to transport her body to the desk. Steeling herself, she glanced down into Reese's smiling face and felt her stomach drop six inches.

Reese's left arm was draped casually around the shoulders of a slender, dark-haired woman. Kristel? Laney couldn't tell much about the woman from the photo. Her hair was pulled back into a sleek ponytail and a pair of designer sunglasses concealed her eyes. Nonplussed, Laney noted the picture had been taken on board a cruise ship—to Alaska? She could see snow-capped mountains in the background. Had they gone to Alaska on their honeymoon?

Laney closed her eyes against the influx of pain this realization caused. But the steadying weight of two warm hands on her shoulders acted as a filter to those feelings, dulling them before they could cut any deeper. *Ben.* She could feel the heat of his body inches from her own. Could smell the tangy down-to-earth scent of his cologne.

"She's not half as pretty as you are," he whispered in her ear, his breath stirring her hair. Laney found herself fighting the temptation to lean into him. To absorb all his common sense and strength into her body. Did he really think she was pretty? Suddenly the knowledge that Ben found her attractive mattered a whole lot more to her than where her husband had honeymooned with another woman. But she had to find answers for Josh.

Laney drew her eyes away from the photo and opened the top drawer, hoping to find an address book or something that might give her the names of Graham's friends and associates, who could provide a less biased appraisal of Graham's relations with Kristel, Nelson and Dallyn. Reese had always used an electronic notebook. Maybe he'd still retained the habit, even though he'd lost his memory.

The top drawer didn't hold anything of interest. Just pens, notepads, elastic bands and paper clips. She tried the bottom filing drawer. It was empty. "Looks like Dallyn was right and Graham didn't do any real work," she told Ben in a low tone.

"Try the middle drawer," Ben urged.

"I think not," said a cold voice from the doorway. Laney started guiltily and felt a hot wave of embarrassment swell from her chest to her face as she met the censure in Dallyn's eyes.

"I'm afraid you've overstayed your welcome and I'm going to have to ask you to leave."

She wiped her damp palms on her jeans. "I'm sorry, we were just—"

Dallyn cut her off. "I'm really not interested in hearing your apologies. I've answered your questions to the best of my ability, but my generosity ends at trespassing. Now, please leave or I'll call the police. I'm sure they'd be interested to know you were rifling through Graham's office. Perhaps I'll call them anyway."

"There's no need to call the police," Ben said passively. "Mrs. Dobson has every right to enter her husband's office."

"Not until the police confirm Graham's identity and, even then, not without Kristel's permission," Dallyn replied stiffly.

"But something here may help us prove Graham Walker was also Reese Dobson," Laney argued.

"I doubt that. An officer was here earlier and helped himself to whatever he thought might be of assistance to the police in finding Graham's murderer."

"Oh." Laney hadn't thought of that. Of course, the police would have already been here.

Dallyn gripped the brass doorknob and stood to one side so they could pass. "I'll see you out."

"THAT WAS ENLIGHTENING," Ben quipped, glancing at Laney in concern as they emerged from the office building onto Denman Street. She'd been bombarded with a steady stream of unpleasant facts since they'd found Reese, and so far she'd held up like a trooper, but he was worried about how much more she could take.

"What?" Laney replied with a distracted air. A chilly breeze blew in from the white-capped waters of English Bay and whipped her auburn hair around her face.

Aware they might be under police surveillance, but not giving a damn anyway, Ben tucked his arm securely around Laney's shoulders and guided her in the direction of the rental car.

"Dallyn said Graham had inherited some money from a grandmother. Where do you think Reese got the money to invest in the company?" he asked. "Presumably, if he had amnesia, he lost all his ID. So, where did he get the money?"

"Oh, my God, I never thought of that. You're right."

"He must have—" Ben paused, stopping short of voicing his suspicions. Laney would only resent him for it. He darted a glance at her pale profile. Her lips were clamped tightly together. Her cheeks looked as if they'd been sculpted from ice, but were red from the cold. With a rush of empathy, he realized that sooner or later she would reach the same conclusions on her own, when she was ready. And he loved her all the more for her tenacious loyalty to Reese—however undeserved.

"Reese must have what, Ben? Invested in the stock market?" The edge in her voice was unmistakable.

She tried to curtail the hair fluttering around her face by tucking it behind her ears.

"Yes," he lied, using the excuse of opening the passenger door of the rental car to keep his gaze averted from her.

She shot him an accusing glance as she climbed into the car. The wind whipped at her words. "You don't have to try to protect me, Ben. With Reese's experience as an analyst and all those on-site visits he's conducted over the years to companies his firm considered potential investments, it's only logical that he might unwittingly use some of the insider knowledge he'd picked up. He probably made a killing in the stock market, which is why he was only playing at being in the import/export business." Her eyes glittered as she reached out and prevented him from closing the door. "I need you to be honest with me, Ben. Even if you think it'll hurt me."

Ben stood on the curb staring down at her, the open car door between them adding to the awkwardness. She wanted honesty? He glanced at the Vancouverites hurrying down the sidewalk, coats buttoned up to their chins, their heads bent into the wind, then glanced back at Laney. She was still waiting for an answer. But a sidewalk seemed an inappropriate place to tell her he was in love with her. Or what he really thought of her husband. The man had just died the day before and it seemed selfish to confront Laney with his feelings when she was reeling with grief. Still, he sensed a distinctive this-is-a-relationship-test ring to the conversation and he was damned if he'd fail.

Swallowing hard, he closed the door and marched around to the driver's side. Laney's scent, fragrant as a hothouse bloom, mingled with the damp, salt-laden air in the confines of the compact sedan as he slid onto the seat and faced her. A bubble of tension expanded in his chest. The desire to touch her tingled in his cold fingers, but he knew she wanted the truth, not comfort.

"What if Reese really didn't have amnesia? What if he faked his death so he could use insider information to make a fortune?" he asked softly.

Her eyes widened and her shallow gasp made him wince.

Then she nodded and squared her shoulders. But her chin wavered as she plucked a piece of lint from the sleeve of her jacket and said in a small, tight voice, "It's killing me to think he lied to me. How can I tell Josh his father did something so dishonest?"

Relief that she hadn't turned on him for questioning Reese's ethics eased some of the tension expanding in a thick balloon against his ribs, but Ben's hands trembled on his thighs. He drew a deep breath. "First of all, we're merely speculating," he said almost gruffly, wondering why he'd never felt this insane fluctuation in emotions when he'd fallen in love with Rebecca. Maybe it was because her death had changed him, had completely stripped him from the complacency of ever taking life for granted. "But regardless of what we unearth about Reese," he went on after a moment, "I have no doubts whatsoever that you'll find the right words for Josh. You always seem to know what to say to Scott. You're the only adult he talks to besides my mother and me, and his teacher. And look how you convinced Nelson to try to arrange an interview with Kristel.''

She shook her head, denying his arguments. "We don't know if Kristel will see us yet. And even if she does agree, it's probably because the police encouraged Nelson to arrange a meeting if we insisted on one." She made a wry face. "They probably think we're holding off with our blackmail demand until we're face-to-face."

Ben squelched the urge to rebut her demurral with a bolstering kiss that would melt the condensation fogging up the windows. "Don't sell yourself short. I think Butterfield discarded that notion within a few minutes of meeting you," he replied, wondering how a genuinely warm and compassionate woman like Laney could ever doubt her worth or her effect on others. Or the effect she had on him. Heat seared his groin with the blasting intensity of a furnace.

Ben glanced at the digital clock on the dash, seeking an acceptable excuse to escape the enforced intimacy of the car—and his feelings for her. He scanned the funky, modern West Coast facades of the cafés, video stores, bakeries and espresso bars lining Denman Street. "It's almost five. I'll go scout out a pay phone so we can call Nelson." Ben checked his pockets for a quarter.

"Wait, I'll come with you," Laney said, scrambling out of the car with him. "I want to call Josh and wish him good-night. It's eight o'clock in Ottawa. Your mom should be getting the boys ready for bed."

Ben valiantly tried to come up with a reason to

prevent her from tagging along, but her obvious eagerness to talk to Josh seemed vastly more important than his need to allow his male urges to return to a state of hibernation. One look at her earnest expression obliterated the half dozen cop-outs forming in his mind. A huge, red-foil heart, part of a Valentine display in the storefront window behind her, framed her petite figure—her tiny booted feet, jeans that snugly clung to her shapely calves and hips, and the V where the zipper of her mauve jacket had nudged down to reveal the bright purple-and-yellow petals of a pansy. Blood pounded in his ears in heavy, scorching waves. The pure, natural whimsy of her appearance pushed him to the brink of a complete and total meltdown.

The jarring honk of a car horn sliced into his consciousness. Drawing a ragged breath, Ben made a discreet adjustment to the front of his brown corduroys and prayed that the answers they were seeking would come fast and easy as he joined her on the sidewalk.

Then he could devote all his time and energy toward convincing Laney that love and marriage could be spectacular the second time around.

Chapter Seven

"Are you sure this is the right place?" Laney asked anxiously as they drove into an almost deserted parking lot near the West Vancouver waterfront.

"The sign said John Lawson Park," Ben remarked, cutting the engine. "We're supposed to leave the car here and walk down the lane to the entrance to the Seawalk. There's a back gate we can use to get on the grounds so we don't have to weed through the journalists hounding the street entrance."

Laney nodded vaguely, staring at a row of evergreens that gave the parking lot an air of isolation, and mustered up her courage for a face-to-face meeting with her husband's other wife. They'd gotten caught in the rush-hour traffic inching over the Lions Gate Bridge at a snail's pace. There probably wasn't a more picturesque place in the world for a traffic jam. But the splendor of the North Shore Mountains rising magnificently from the shoreline of the Burrard Inlet, their lofty shoulders draped with snowy shawls, had deepened the ache growing in her heart. The famous twin peaks, known as the Lions, had seemed to survey and protect the wealthy enclave of West Vancouver, which curled in an indolent crescent along the deep blue waters of the inlet to the west.

Reese had referred to Vancouver once as Lotus-land—the land of contentment, beautiful from sea to sky. Had he lived a life of contentment as Graham Walker with Kristel before his murder?

Did she really want to know? A sick lump of fear nested in her stomach as she continued to stare out the windshield, unable to move.

She swallowed hard as a sudden longing for Josh welled within her. Their call had been far too brief, and she'd let him do most of the talking because she was afraid he might be able to tell by her voice that something was wrong. But she felt much better knowing he was happy in Georgina's care.

"Ready?" Ben asked her.

"As ready as I'll ever be," she replied stiffly.

They crossed a set of railroad tracks to reach the lane. Laney noted almost dully the leaded-glass windows and artful touches trimming the quaint cottages tucked beneath the dark, sweeping branches of fir and cedar trees.

"Where's the house?" she asked Ben, struggling to keep up with his long strides as they turned onto the Seawalk. Apartment towers lined the shore here, thousands of windows angled toward the view. Waves crashed against the rocks butting the asphalt walkway and dampened her face with a fine mist. In the distance, Vancouver Island resembled a huddled sleeping form.

Ben glanced down at her and Laney felt her heart give a peculiar leap as his blue-black eyes noticeably softened. His midnight hair ruffled the worn collar of his brown leather jacket. His pace slowed to match hers and Laney had an insane desire to tuck her hand in the crook of his elbow and follow the shimmering rosy path that beamed across the water, straight from the heart of a glorious salmon-and-gold sunset. But to do so would be a sheer act of denial in the worst way. Not to mention that Ben quite likely had a lady friend he'd prefer to share a sunset with.

"Nelson said the house is located several lots east of an apartment building that resembles a pink birthday cake decorated with icing. We're to look for a distinctive privacy fence. There's a gate hidden in it and he'll unlock it for us."

Laney nodded mutely and feigned great interest in some stones embedded in the path in the shape of a fish. She nearly bumped into an elderly gent as he stopped directly in front of her to unleash a butterscotch Airedale. The animal obediently bounded up to the dog path that was separated from the Seawalk by a chain link fence. Laney thought Josh and Scott would get a kick out of the stick-figure drawings on the sign posted at the entrance to the dog path that showed humans and canines their respective recreational areas.

After they'd walked for several minutes in silence, Ben gestured toward a weathered cedar fence treated with a transparent blue stain. "That's the fence we're looking for." He led her off the Seawalk and up a couple of steps where they could cross over the railroad tracks. Laney reluctantly followed him up a narrow winding trail that took them alongside the fence.

She didn't see any sign of a gate. She half hoped Nelson had made it up.

Ben reached up and twisted a Gothic finial trimming the third fence post from the left. "Now this is a masterpiece of engineering and craftsmanship," he exclaimed as the section of fence opened smoothly.

He peered, as though intrigued, at the hinge mechanism, then flashed her a sheepish grin as he realized what he was doing. "Sorry."

Laney rolled her eyes, unable to resist his contrite expression, which reminded her so much of his son Scott. "It's okay," she assured him, venturing onto the gray brick path that wound through clumps of rhododendrons and azaleas toward a terrace at the back of the house. "Since we haven't been able to drive past a bridge, dam or stadium without your giving them a curious perusal, I'm beginning to accept this as a quirk of your personality."

She lowered her voice, even though there wasn't another soul in sight. "Not to mention that I'm exceedingly grateful for any excuse to postpone our face-off with Kristel for at least another ten seconds."

Ben laughed. "Not looking forward to it, are you?"

"I'd rather clean out my basement. Or dust the medallion in my living-room ceiling with a cotton swab."

She felt Ben's fingers settle on her elbow and give it a faint squeeze as he drew abreast of her. "Smile, we're on camera," he murmured in her ear. "There, on the pole holding the birdhouse. It's probably part of the security system."

Cramps flexed in Laney's stomach at the idea that Kristel might be observing her now—perhaps had even heard the remarks she'd just made. Nelson's timely emergence from a French door at the back of the house, as if on cue, seemed to confirm their progress was being monitored.

"I see you didn't have any trouble with the directions," the car dealership owner said briskly as they joined him on the terrace. Laney thought he appeared distinctly ill at ease. His right foot tapped nervously on the brick pavers and a worried frown creased his narrow brow. "Please come inside... God only knows if there are photographers lurking in the shrubbery."

In alarm, Laney looked back anxiously over her shoulder and scoured the garden. Surely anyone could be concealed behind the dense evergreens? A shudder passed through her. Ben squeezed her elbow again and she glanced at him briefly to exchange a look of encouragement before she took a deep breath and entered into Kristel and Graham's house.

They stepped directly into a spacious living room. A maid in a black-and-white uniform took their coats and hung them in an antique armoire near the door. The pretentiousness and sterile feel of the room jarred Laney's nerves. The sleek sofas and dainty side chairs dared anyone to make themselves too comfortable for any length of time. It seemed a room designed only for entertaining and displaying the exquisite oil paintings mounted on the pale lemon walls. Laney found her eyes drawn to the vases of lilies and white roses that sat atop the grand piano in an alcove at the far end of the room. The vases enshrined a cluster of

framed photographs, each frame a work of art in itself.

She instinctively took a step closer toward them,
but halted in mid-stride at the discreet sound of a
woman clearing her throat. Laney followed the sound
to the graceful figure of a young woman seated in a
delicately wrought gilt armchair positioned near the
window in the alcove. Kristel Walker, she presumed.

Clothed in an elegant black pantsuit, the woman
was a stark portrait of a grieving widow. Her hair fell
in a curtain to her shoulders—its glossy darkness em-
phasizing the violet smudges of exhaustion highlight-
ing her cheekbones and the fragility of her fine-boned
features.

Her only noticeable resemblance to her brother was
her spare build and her unapproachable aura. The
chair she sat in reminded Laney of a throne as she
absorbed the overt hostility burning in Kristel's hazel
eyes and felt an answering response of resentment
flare with a flurry deep inside her. Laney clamped her
lips together and counted to ten slowly. A heated con-
frontation with Kristel wouldn't help matters.

And, strange as it seemed, Laney understood Kristel's fury. Laney remembered all too well the shock
and anger she'd experienced when she'd been informed of Reese's death in the avalanche. The numbing sense of grief and the terrible fear of how she was
going to cope without him. She was still coming to
grips with the trauma of having him return from the
dead only to be taken from her again. Someday she
prayed she'd be able to make it through a day without
envisioning that house and Reese propped up in that

bed. The thought that Reese might have betrayed her was eating her up inside, incessantly nibbling at the underpinnings of their life together and the memories that she held most dear.

She fervently hoped Kristel would be as keen to ferret out answers as she was—no matter how painful it would be for both of them.

"Kristel, this is Laney Dobson," Nelson said, going to stand by his sister's chair like a courtier who'd dispatched his duty.

Laney gave him a nod of appreciative thanks and fumbled in her purse for the family photos she always carried in her wallet. "Thank you for seeing me," she began, her voice shaking. "I realize this is terribly difficult and awkward for you—it is for me, too. My husband Reese was a financial analyst. He died in an avalanche here in Whistler fourteen months ago...." Slowly, stumbling, the words came describing the accident, the arrival of the anniversary card, and the valentine she had received from Reese two weeks ago.

"Reese didn't show up at the restaurant—probably because he spotted Ben. As the police may have told you, a woman gave me the address where to meet him. When I arrived, I found him upstairs. I tried to give him mouth-to-mouth resuscitation, but he was already dead."

Kristel remained stonily silent. Laney had the disquieting thought that either Kristel or her brother could have been the killer. Or have hired someone to do their bidding.

Removing a photo of Reese from a plastic protective sleeve, Laney passed it to the other woman. "This was my husband."

Kristel reluctantly took it. Her gasp of surprise as she gazed down at the photograph reverberated in the room. "Oh, my God," she whispered. "He does look like Graham." A tear slipped onto her cheek and trickled down her face.

Laney felt tears gather in her own eyes. A hot lump of doubt churned beneath her ribs as she handed Kristel another photo. "This is our son, Josh. He's nine now."

Kristel studied the photo and handed it back without comment, but Laney could see that the dark-haired woman's jaw trembled violently.

Laney straightened her spine determinedly. "The only explanation I can come up with…is that Reese must have suffered amnesia in the accident and taken on a new identity. I think he recently got his memory back and wasn't sure how to deal with the situation, so he invited me to meet him here."

Kristel shifted suddenly in her chair and cast a cautious glance at her brother. "What do you think, Nelson? I have to admit M-Mrs. Dobson's suggestion makes sense in an odd sort of way." Her tone altered, taking on the grating sharpness of glass. "And it gives her all the more reason to have killed Graham. She was probably furious when Graham told her he was married to someone else."

Laney's mouth dropped open and she saw a haze of red. What made this woman think she had the right to make accusations? Laney clenched her hands so tightly at her sides that her knuckles throbbed as she struggled to retain her dignity. She noticed Ben had tensed beside her, his jaw set like a bulldog's ready to leap to her defense. It made her feel better that Kristel irritated him, too. But this was her battle and she was going to fend for herself. "I don't blame you for your suspicions. I'd be a liar if I claimed I haven't entertained a suspicion or two concerning your involvement in Reese's murder."

"How dare you—"

"Ladies, please," Nelson cut in, dropping a placating hand on his sister's shoulder. "I think it would be in everyone's best interests if we all calm down and try to share information to see what we can piece together. Kristel, Mrs. Dobson asked me when you met Graham, but I wasn't sure exactly."

Kristel flushed scarlet but answered the question. "We met at the end of March, at a charity gala on Grouse Mountain to raise funds for a local women's shelter. I was in charge of organizing the door prizes for the dinner…and somehow or other, the name of Graham's company was passed along to me. There were a number of corporate sponsors and financial institutions involved." She looked down at her French-manicured hands. "I talked to Graham a couple of times by phone, but I didn't actually meet him until that night. He gave me a call the following morning and asked me out for lunch."

Laney nodded. "Well, that certainly seems to substantiate my theory. I'm curious what Graham told you about his background. Dallyn Vohringer tells us Graham had used an inheritance from a grandmother to fund Connoisseur Specialty Wines?"

"He told me he was an only child—born in Brandon, Manitoba. In fact, the grandmother he inherited the money from lived in Brandon. Her name was Millie Walker, I believe. She owned a furniture store. She raised him after his parents died in a car accident when he was in his teens. Apparently, they were hit by a train. It was very sad. Graham didn't like talking about it."

Laney tried to make sense out of what Kristel was saying. "Reese's parents divorced when he was six. He never saw his father again after that. His mother died when he was in university. There was no one in his family named Millie that I know of. Do you think he simply invented a past? Maybe it's something he read in a novel or remembered from a movie."

She walked toward the pictures on the gleaming black surface of the piano. "May I?" she said, seeking permission to touch them.

"Of course," Kristel replied tightly.

Laney felt her knees wobble unsteadily as the images in the photos lambasted her heart. Reese's familiar grin. Kristel's contented smile. The playful and formal poses. The obvious attraction between them. She was grateful she'd faced the initial shock of seeing Reese with his arms around another woman in the privacy of Graham's office. For some reason, hearing Kristel refer to him as "Graham" allowed her to put some distance between her feelings for Reese and the man who'd married Kristel.

"Did Graham play the stock market?" she asked, finding that she could speak past the hurt that burned in her throat.

"Not that I'm aware of. But before we were married, we agreed our financial situations would be completely separate—mostly to make my brother happy. We both signed a prenuptial agreement, mainly to keep Nelson from voicing any kind of objection during the wedding ceremony." A wistful smile touched her lips. "Frankly, it was not a topic of great importance between us. And we forgave Nelson for interfering and acting like an overprotective big brother."

She rose from the chair and joined Laney at the piano. Kristel was tall enough to be a runway model and Laney instantly felt dwarfed by her. Kristel lovingly picked up a heavy crystal frame that held a photo of Graham carrying her over the threshold of the house. "Nelson's wife, Sandy, took this one when we came back from our two-week honeymoon in France."

Laney noticed dully that Kristel had managed to talk her husband into wearing a wide gold wedding band. Reese had never worn one. Nor was he wearing his favorite watch. Had he lost it in the avalanche? Or was it possible this was a case of mistaken identity and someone just wanted her to think Graham Walker was Reese? Something niggled at the back of Laney's mind but she couldn't draw it forward.

"What about Graham's friends?" she asked. "Perhaps I could talk to some of them. They might know more about Graham's background—or have some idea who may have wanted to kill him."

"No." Kristel replaced the photograph on the piano and aligned it just so with the tips of her fingers. "I would prefer to let the police handle this." She shot Laney a warning glance. "To be quite honest, I find your timing rather ironic. If you loved him so much, why didn't you search more thoroughly for him when he originally went missing? I think you're covering your tracks because your boyfriend nearly caught you in the act."

Laney bristled as though she'd been slapped. Anger turned her words to ice as she tried to explain. "There weren't any tracks or signs discovered in the snow that would give anyone reason to hope he might have escaped the avalanche. The authorities traced his beeper signal to the crevasse and tried in vain to reach him. But tell me, why did you agree to meet me if you had no intention of assisting in the investigation? Was it curiosity?"

Laney felt her temper skyrocket as Kristel looked down her long, slim nose at her.

"Hardly. I'd hoped we could come to some agreement about Graham's burial arrangements. But perhaps it would be better done through our respective lawyers."

Laney's chin shot up a notch—anything to give her an extra millimeter or two of height against this towering, sanctimonious snob. "I laid *my husband* to rest on Mount Currie over a year ago. How and where you wish to lay *your Graham* to rest is entirely your own decision." Turning abruptly on her heel, Laney marched out of the house.

She'd have gone out the front door if she'd known where it was located. The fact she was slinking out a back entrance infuriated her. She heard Ben make some kind of parting remark, but she had no idea what he said. The blood was pounding too ferociously in her ears as she ran across the terrace and onto the lawn.

The backyard was swathed in the shadows of the descending night, but the path to the fence was illuminated. Still, she cursed under her breath when she reached the fence and discovered she was too short to activate the latch for the gate. Determined not to let the gate stop her, she jumped up and managed to twist the finial.

Leaving the gate open for Ben, she made a beeline for the Seawalk, nearly tripping on the uneven ground. Her pace increased once she'd crossed the railroad tracks and leapt down the stone steps. She had no idea where the car was parked and she didn't care. She just needed to move. To release the anger and her pent-up feelings into the cool air and the crashing of the waves against the rocks.

Footsteps thundered on the asphalt path behind her. "Wait up, Laney," she heard Ben call. "Where are you going?"

"Anywhere. As far away from *that woman* as I can get," she shouted over her shoulder.

Ben caught up with her and handed her her jacket. "Here, you forgot this."

She took it gratefully, tears stinging her eyes at his kindness. She jammed her arms into the sleeves without missing a step, terrified she'd fall apart if she let herself stand still. Ben kept pace with her silently, his head bowed. "How could Reese have loved her, Ben?" she demanded, ignoring the zipper. "She isn't anything like me. Look at that house she lives in—

and her life. She looked down her nose at me, like I was pond scum. And she's so *tall!*''

Ben lifted his head, his expression solemn. ''Do you think you could only love someone exactly like Reese? 'Cause I'll tell you, if that's the case, you'll probably spend the rest of your life alone. When I started dating after Rebecca passed away, I tried very hard to find someone like her. But where do you find someone who grows mountains of zucchini so she can pass it all over the neighborhood, has cravings for strawberry yogurt at 3:00 a.m., is afraid of the sound Velcro makes when it rips, and writes down every cent she ever spent in a ledger?''

His voice grew husky and raw. Laney could barely hear it over the sound of the sea. ''I met a few women who vaguely resembled her. Or liked gardening or were devout penny-pinchers. But there was no chemistry. It took me a while to realize that I wasn't ever going to find anyone like Rebecca—to even try seemed to me to minimize her uniqueness as an individual.'' He laced his fingers through Laney's and she felt a tingle race up her arm. How was it that she always seemed to connect with him on some basic, elemental level? ''Now all I want is purely unscientific magic that lasts longer than three dates.''

He tugged gently on her hand, causing her to draw up short. ''Stop. I want to tell you something and I want you to listen.'' His other hand cupped her chin and forced it upward until their gazes locked. Alarm tumbled in somersaults in her stomach at the tight lines bracketing his mouth and the deep, black heat in his eyes that seemed wilder than the wind and as unfathomable as the dark water lifting and pounding against the shore. Laney couldn't move, couldn't breathe, spellbound by the callused warmth of the fingertips stroking her chin.

"In my humble opinion," he said with a sexy growl, "you're a beautiful, loving woman and it was Reese's misfortune that the avalanche caused him to lose his memories of you. Because you are definitely memorable."

Laney stared up at him and blinked away a hot flood of tears as his words hit home and rubbed out the burrs of insecurities clinging to her heart. "Oh, Ben, thank you," she murmured. "You really know how to make a girl feel good."

Impulsively, she rose on tiptoe, intending to kiss his cheek. But Ben angled her chin toward his mouth and within the beat of a pulse, Laney knew from the determined look in his eyes that he was going to kiss her. On the lips. Uncertainty and anticipation snapped her nerve endings to a full state of alert as he lowered his head and brushed his mouth against hers.

Laney stifled a moan as the fiery heat generated by the tentative joining of their mouths cut through her like a jagged spear of lightning and literally knocked her off her toes—abruptly ending the kiss.

Ben, with the split-second timing and agility of a man who can fly over ice on skates, steadied her and set her on her feet. "Careful."

"I'm so clumsy." Laney felt the embarrassing heat of a blush infiltrate her wind-chilled cheeks and kept her head lowered, terrified at the prospect of meeting his gaze after that kiss. If she did, would he kiss her again? Did she want him to?

There was no question in her mind that he had deliberately kissed her, but for all she knew, he could merely have intended it to be a kiss between friends, part of his pep talk. Ben had certainly given her no sign before that he was interested in her romantically. Now she'd probably never know for sure, because she was vertically challenged!

Silence stretched between them, punctuated by the steady one-two punch of the incoming tide and the rhythmic slap of approaching footsteps.

Ben cleared his throat and Laney leveled her gaze on the bobbing of his Adam's apple, then wished she hadn't. The dark stubble of a five o'clock shadow gave a dangerous and tempting allure to his skin. The need to be held and comforted by him, to touch her tongue to the mysterious contours of his neck and feel the rasp of his beard, welled so strongly in her breast that she closed her eyes and pressed her hand to her mouth. Lord, what was the matter with her?

"Laney—" he began, breaking off suddenly as a pair of female joggers in black leggings and neon jackets skirted them.

"Excuse us, handsome," one of the women puffed, darting a flirtatious smile at Ben. Laney wondered how Rebecca had stood this...women ogling her husband all the time. The fact that Ben had most likely kissed a lot of women made what had just happened between them seem even more insignificant.

"Let's walk," she said with an inward sigh, moving out of the way and lengthening her stride. "We're blocking the path. And I could use the exercise to clear my mind. Then we can find a place for dinner and figure out what we can do next.''

''We'll call McBain from the restaurant. Maybe the police have learned something more that can help us.''

She waited expectantly for him to bring up whatever he'd been about to say earlier, but he remained silent, as though the incident was already forgotten or not worth mentioning again. Laney zipped her jacket up snugly under her chin and told herself that Ben had far too many women in his life for her comfort, anyway.

BEN COULDN'T BELIEVE he'd kissed her. What an idiot! Laney probably thought he was an insensitive jerk. Her husband had died yesterday and her friend was making passes at her. Still, for just a golden moment when their lips had met, Ben had tasted pure magic and thought he could have it all: Laney, love, a complete family again.

The memory of it warmed him body and soul.

Then she'd pulled away from him as if he were a monster, and he knew he'd blown it. She wouldn't even look him in the eye afterward.

Was he a fool to think a relationship could work out between them?

Gripping the steering wheel of the rental car tightly, Ben kept his eyes trained on the Sea to Sky highway as it narrowed from a wide highway to two lanes after Brackendale and the speed limit dropped to accommodate the rocky terrain.

They'd called McBain from the restaurant and had decided to drive back to Whistler tonight because McBain had told them the autopsy and forensic results were in and he wanted to see them tomorrow morning at the Walkers' chalet on Horstman Lane. He'd also advised them of their right to have a lawyer present at the meeting, but Laney told Ben it was ridiculous to waste valuable time seeking out a lawyer when she could be investigating what happened to Reese. But Ben was worried. Did McBain have some incriminating evidence on them—or Laney? Was that why he'd advised them of their rights? Or was it just standard procedure because they were obviously suspects?

Laney was quiet in the passenger seat beside him, her posture stiffer than an oak plank. Their conversation had been stilted over dinner and he'd noticed that she'd only picked at her salmon steak and wild rice.

The headlights of a car loomed up behind them. *Great, someone in a hurry.* Ben put his foot on the brake and slowed into a sharp curve that angled around a knuckle of rock. The car behind him stuck to his bumper, pinning them in the glare of its high beams. Ben swore and hoped there would be a passing lane ahead where the car could safely get by. No such luck. There was another curve.

But to his relief, the car backed off. Then, next thing he knew, he heard the roar of a car engine gunning behind him and noticed the car's headlights swerve left. The jerk wasn't going to try to pass going into a curve, was he?

"Oh, my God, Ben! What's he doing?" Laney cried out in alarm.

"I don't know." Ben braked hard and blared the horn in warning, praying an oncoming car wouldn't emerge from the pitch-black recesses of the blind curve and turn them all into corpses. Fear pumped in his lungs, seconds ticking by with agonizing slowness as he expected the other car to overtake them.

Instead, his head was slammed against the headrest as their rental car was rammed from behind and sent skittering across the lane toward a solid wall of rock.

Chapter Eight

Ben fought for control of the car to avoid hitting the wall head-on. The sound of rubber screeching on asphalt filled his ears as he jerked on the steering wheel.

Steel scraped against stone like nails on a chalkboard and crumpled like an aluminum can as they impacted. Then all he heard was Laney's scream, high-pitched and terrified.

The car bounced and jolted over the rocky debris littering the base of the rock face. Ben managed to get the car back on the road and slowly rounded the curve, every cell in his body primed for danger.

The other car was nowhere in sight.

The road was too narrow to risk stopping here. They could cause an accident. He'd pull over in the first turnoff he could find to check out the car.

"Are you hurt, Laney?" he demanded, reaching over to touch her leg. Her trembling matched his own.

"N-no, I'm fine," she stammered. "Frightened out of my wits, but not hurt."

"Thank goodness."

Laney gripped his arm. "Are you okay?"

"I'm okay." Ben gave her a dopey grin and patted

her knee. At least the accident had got her reaching out to him again. "I don't suppose you happened to get their license plate, did you?"

She shook her head. "No, everything happened so fast I didn't think of it. But it was a two-door sedan— red or burgundy—I saw that much. Two passengers. Probably kids or a drunk driver."

"Yeah, maybe." Ben saw a wide shoulder ahead and pulled off the road. His heart was still thundering and his legs felt like putty as he put the car in neutral and switched on the hazard lights. He left the engine running—just in case.

"What do you mean…maybe?" Laney asked.

He turned on the interior dome light and shifted toward her. Her eyes were huge in her pale face. The knowledge that she might easily have been injured or killed a few minutes ago made him feel as if someone had tried to steal the keystone from his soul.

And the thought made him damn angry.

Ben wet his lips. "You said you didn't want me to lie to you, so I won't. That car hit us on purpose. I think someone is trying to shut us up."

FIFTY MINUTES LATER, Ben heaved a sigh of relief when he unlocked the door of their suite at the Chateau Whistler. All he wanted to do was get Laney inside and call McBain from a secure phone. They'd driven the last forty kilometers without further incident. There'd been no sign of the red sedan along the highway. He'd had the feeling this morning that maybe the police were watching every move they made, but they hadn't come to their aid after the accident. Maybe they'd dropped the tail when it appeared they weren't trying to hit the Butterfields up for some "shush" money.

Or maybe someone else had been tailing them.

Ben wasn't sure who, but the questions he and Laney had been asking were obviously making someone nervous.

He gave Laney a probing look as he reached in to flick on the lights, then held the door for her. She seemed to have shrunk inside her jacket, as though the garment were protective packing for a fragile doll that might shatter into a thousand pieces at any moment.

Ben dropped the two small overnight bags they'd packed in the event their questions necessitated a night's stay in Vancouver on the plush carpet and helped Laney remove her jacket. Her expression told him she was a million miles away. Perhaps lost in her fears?

Something inside him snapped.

He kneaded her shoulders lightly, feeling the stiff coils of tension. "How about a brandy and a bubble bath to help you relax?" he suggested, tamping down a delectable image of Laney luxuriating in the enormous tub in their suite, her auburn hair swept up on top of her head and bubbles caressing her creamy shoulders. "You've had a rough day."

It was all he could do not to fold his arms around her and let out the feelings in his heart.

Laney tilted her head back toward him and crinkled her nose. "That's putting it mildly! It's not every day a woman has a close encounter with her husband's wife and a boulder the size of one of the Gatineau Hills, though I'm not sure which was more traumatic. A bath sounds heavenly, but I'll pass on the brandy. We should call McBain first, though, and report the accident."

"You're right." Ben experienced an overwhelming sense of loss as she stepped away from him and walked into the living area of their suite. He could still sense the delicate warmth of her in his fingers as he shrugged out of his coat and followed her. Boy, he had it bad. He pulled McBain's card out of his wallet. "I'll call if you like."

Her state of fatigue was evident in the soft glow cast by the table lamp. She reached out an unsteady hand for the card. "No, thanks, Ben. I should do it. He was my husband."

Ben hadn't expected her to accept his offer. He'd already learned she'd never delegate a responsibility she felt was her own, no matter how tired she was. But still, he thought he'd heard an extra emphasis in her voice when she'd said *husband* as though she were trying to stretch the word into an impassable line between them.

Which it was.

He kicked himself again for kissing her.

Her phone conversation with Corporal McBain was surprisingly brief. Laney hung up the phone and ran her fingers through her hair. "Looks like my bath will have to wait. Corporal McBain wants to see us—and the car—at the detachment right away. Maybe the accident will finally convince him we didn't have anything to do with Reese's murder."

Ben nodded and gave her a supportive smile. "Yeah. Let's hope." Hope was about all he had to live on these days.

LANEY TAGGED ALONG, worrying her lower lip as Ben and Corporal McBain circled the rental car beneath floodlights in the parking lot. After noting Ben's account of the accident and the location on a form attached to a clipboard, the RCMP officer crouched down to examine the rear bumper.

"You said the sedan hit you here on the left side?"

"Yes," Ben replied, crouching beside him.

"Hmm." McBain peered at the bumper. "There aren't any noticeable marks of an impact," he observed in his booming voice. "The taillights are intact. Were there any witnesses to the accident other than yourselves?"

Ben shook his head.

McBain scrawled something on the form, then rose and walked to the right side of the rental car. Ben and Laney followed him.

The considerable amount of time McBain took to examine the damage to the body of the vehicle made Laney uneasy. She took a deep breath, filling her lungs with cold, fresh air and hopped from one foot to the other in an effort to stay warm.

McBain straightened. "Well, you definitely came in contact with some rock here. You're lucky you both escaped without injury. It's unfortunate you didn't contact us as soon as the accident occurred. We might have stood a better chance of catching the other driver." The underlying hint of disapproval in the corporal's statement was unmistakable.

Ben, however, shrugged it off. "Yeah, well, the idea of searching for a pay phone in the middle of nowhere made me feel like a sitting duck. I wanted a lot of lights and a lot of people."

McBain's expression was unreadable. "In any case, we'll do our best to find the car that hit you. If you remember anything more about the car or its occupants, don't hesitate to speak up." He tore off a copy of the accident report form and handed it to Ben. "You should give your rental-car agency a call first thing in the morning."

"Corporal," Laney said, clearing her throat. "I appreciate your seeing us this late. But you don't seem to be lending much weight to the possibility that someone ran us off the road on purpose. My meeting with Mrs. Walker wasn't exactly a tea party. Come to think of it, Dallyn Vohringer came close to kicking us out of his office this afternoon. He mentioned an officer had gone through Graham's desk drawers this morning. Did the officer find anything that could shed some light on the murder?"

"Nothing that appears to be of importance as yet," McBain said carefully. "But we're still in the early stages of the investigation and we aren't ruling out any theories—or anyone as a potential suspect."

"Well, what about the fingerprint check?" Laney pushed. "Have you gotten confirmation that Reese and Graham are the same man?"

"Unfortunately no. But then, I really wasn't expecting them until tomorrow morning."

Laney pressed her palms together to prevent herself
from tearing her hair out in clumps. "I see. Since
we're here, maybe you can share the results of the
autopsy and forensic tests now. Were they able to
estimate a time of death?"

"Yes, they were, but I'd prefer to hold off discussing this with you until after the walk-through tomorrow. You're a key witness and the best way you
can assist us in catching Graham Walker's killer is
by helping us clarify your movements in the house. I
don't want any test results altering your recollection
of what happened." McBain lightly touched her
shoulder. "You'll know more in the morning. I promise."

Laney shuddered and moved out of his reach.
McBain's promise had an ominous ring to it.

McBAIN PROVED he was a man of his word. As soon
as Laney and Ben met with him, Constable Henry and
another uniformed corporal in the circular drive outside the house on Horstman Lane, McBain informed
her they'd heard back from Ottawa on the fingerprint
check.

After thirty-six hours of waiting and wondering if
Graham and Reese were the same person, it struck
her as being a cruel and unjust punishment that she
should be told there was no record, and that she must
endure another delay of days or weeks until a positive
identification could be made.

Laney stared numbly as a melting clump of snow
shifted off the tip of a cedar bough and thudded softly
to the ground. A gray mist had settled over the Whist-

ler valley overnight, bringing with it a light rainfall that added a dusting of snow to the ski runs at the top of the mountains where the temperature was several degrees colder. "We've already put a call through to your husband's dentist. They're sending Reese's dental records by overnight courier," McBain told her. He gestured toward the other corporal, who nodded solemnly and raised a video camera to his eye to begin filming. "Corporal Axworthy is with the Ident team. He'll be recording the walk-through on film."

Corporal McBain advised them both of their right to have a lawyer present again, which they both waived, then he led them toward the front door. "We'll begin here, Mrs. Dobson," he instructed. A rivulet of rain dribbled off the brim of his forage cap. "Never mind the camera, just talk to me. What time did you arrive at the house?"

Laney glanced uncertainly at the camera, then back at Corporal McBain. "About ten after six. I checked my watch as I climbed onto the front porch to see how early I was. I wasn't supposed to meet Reese until seven."

"What did you do next? Ring the bell?"

"No, I didn't ring the bell. The door was ajar a few inches. I saw the candlelight and the rose petals on the floor." Conscious of her attentive audience and the camera, Laney went through the motions of opening the door and removing her coat and shoes in the foyer. The men removed their coats, as well, and wiped their feet.

The air in the house was as stagnant as the inside

of a tomb. Laney felt the somber atmosphere hem her in as though she were being measured for a shroud. Ben's face was a tight mask of concentration. Moisture gleamed on his cheeks and hair. She noticed he had the same aversion as she to stepping on the withered rose petals still littering the floor. McBain and Constable Henry, however, looked ready to pounce on every word she said.

She led the way into the dining room and stopped behind one of the chairs drawn up to the dining-room table. The room looked much as it had the other night, without the luster of the candlelight. And, in the gray morning light, Laney could see the grains of a black powder on the pale wood of the table.

"Did you sit down at the table?" McBain asked.

Laney shook her head. "No. I smelled food cooking, which made me think Reese might be in the kitchen, so I tried to find the kitchen."

"Did you touch anything on the table?"

Laney frowned. "I don't believe so. I might have touched the chair. I'm not sure."

"We found your fingerprints on the chair and the silverware. Henry, show her the silverware."

Laney felt a chord of alarm vibrate through her as Constable Henry produced a sealed plastic bag containing the silverware from a large black briefcase he carried with him. His young face looked grave. Laney couldn't understand why they were making such a fuss about a knife, a fork and a spoon. Ben seemed equally puzzled. "Well, I don't recall touching it. But maybe I forgot I did. I certainly didn't set the table or sit down, if that's what you're implying."

"Let's continue on," McBain instructed loudly. "Where did you go next?" Laney led them into the kitchen and explained how she'd opened the oven and seen the cartons of Chinese food. "It occurred to me that Reese might be waiting for me upstairs," she admitted with a blush. "I called out for him to answer me, but he didn't." Laney threaded her way through the house to the staircase, wincing at the clomping sound the men's footsteps made on the granite steps as they mounted the stairs behind her. The sound echoed in the still house and made her feel as if an army were in pursuit of her. She stopped on the second-floor landing and faced Corporal McBain.

"When I got upstairs, I could see the glow of candles and the light from the fire through the glass doors. Then I opened the door and I saw…h-him."

"Walk us through your movements."

Laney closed her eyes and swallowed hard, trying to remember the tiniest details of that night. But how she wanted to forget the sight of Reese in that bed! So much blood! Her knees wobbled as she found the courage to open the glass door and enter the bedroom. She couldn't bring herself to focus directly on the bed. But in her peripheral vision, she noted to her relief that the bed had been stripped and the blood-soaked parts of the mattress cut away by the forensics team.

"I ran over to him," she said shakily. "There was blood everywhere. I touched his face. He felt warm and I thought he was still alive, so I ran into the bathroom to get a towel to stop the bleeding." Hugging herself, she walked into the bathroom and pointed at the towel bar near one of the twin sinks.

"You didn't touch anything else or go back into the bathroom for any other reason?" the corporal asked.

"N-no. I went back into the bedroom and wrapped the towel around the wound. I took a first-aid course when my son was a baby so I knew not to try to remove the…" She faltered, not quite sure how to describe the murder weapon. "Anyway, that's when I noticed Reese wasn't breathing and I started artificial respiration."

"Did it occur to you to call 911?"

"Yes, it did." Laney felt her knees wobble. "But I thought it was more important to get some air into Reese's lungs first. That's when Ben arrived and I told him to call for an ambulance."

Laney gave a tiny sigh of relief as McBain turned his steely eyed gaze on Ben.

"What time did you arrive, Mr. Forbes?"

"I honestly don't know," Ben admitted. "Six twenty-five, maybe six-thirty. I got back to the hotel just before six. The concierge told me Laney had asked directions to Horstman Lane. I headed over here in a hurry and parked at the top of the road and started knocking on doors. I went to two houses before I heard a scream and I just started running. I rang the doorbell, but I didn't wait for anyone to answer. I just knew Laney was in here. The door wasn't locked. As soon as I opened it, I heard her crying. I think I called out her name as I came up the stairs and saw her with Reese on the bed—I'm not sure.

She was giving Reese artificial respiration. As soon as she saw me, she told me to call 911.''

McBain nodded and checked his notebook. ''That seems to fit. The call was logged in at 6:33 p.m. What'd you do after you called?''

''I went to assist Laney. Reese didn't have a pulse. It seemed obvious to me he was dead,'' Ben replied matter-of-fact.

''What was the state of the coverings on the bed when you arrived?'' McBain asked Ben.

Ben frowned and Laney saw him glance at the mutilated bed as though trying to stimulate his memory. Laney wondered what in the world McBain was driving at.

''I think the covers were folded back onto the left side of the bed as though Laney flipped them back to examine Reese's injury,'' Ben said after a pause.

''I did push them aside,'' Laney admitted. ''And I pulled the pillows out from behind him and threw them on the rug so I could see if he was breathing.''

McBain addressed Ben. ''Was the left side of the bed fairly neatly made or mussed up when you entered?''

''Neatly made. The top sheet was turned down over the covers like you see in displays in a bedding department. My wife used to do that when she made our bed. Is this really important?''

McBain disregarded Ben's question with a wave of his hand. Laney felt a needle of tension nose sharply up her spine. ''In your attempts to administer first aid to the victim after Mr. Forbes's arrival, did either of you adjust the covers?''

A hot lump swelled in Laney's throat. "After I realized he was gone, I, um, covered him up to his chest. But I still don't understand what the position of the covers has to do with anything."

"I'm getting to that." McBain moved to a spot near the bed. "We've been able to determine that Mr. Walker was standing here, with his back to the bed when he was stabbed. He fell onto the bed and bled to death very quickly. Then his killer propped him up in bed and arranged the coverings around him." McBain walked around the foot of the bed to the left side and gestured with his arms. "The left side of the bed is made up. Pillows plumped nice and pretty. People tend to shed hair and fabric fibers when they're nervous. The Ident team picked up a couple of red hairs on the right side of the bed in the vicinity of Mr. Walker's body. But what we can't figure out is how three red hairs could be found elsewhere in the bed. One was found between the sheets near the foot of the bed. A second was found sandwiched between a blanket and the top sheet, and a third hair was found on a pillow slip on the left side of the bed. On the bottom pillow, actually. There were two on that side of the bed."

Laney's eyes widened in mute shock as she came to the frightening conclusion that McBain thought she'd laid her head on that pillow before she'd killed Reese—lured him to his death with sex. Nausea rose in her throat.

She cast a wary glance at Ben's reflection in the mirror. His brows were drawn into dark slashes over his eyes, mimicking the tight fold of his arms across his denim-clad chest.

Was he buying the corporal's logic?

Ben's lower jaw jutted out. "So what? Couldn't the hairs have been somehow transported when your men were going over the room or when Mr. Walker's body was moved?"

"Well, that could be." McBain's voice sounded as if he doubted it.

Laney choked back the taste of bile, heartened by Ben's steadfast support. "How do you even know it's my hair?" she stammered. "I'm sure I'm not the only redhead in the world. Someone could have planted those red hairs to incriminate me."

"That's certainly possible," McBain coolly agreed. "We'd need a hair sample to confirm it."

"Well, I'll be happy to provide one," Laney said staunchly, with heated indignation. "Because I have nothing to hide."

"I'm glad you feel that way, because we found two other items in the bathroom which trouble me. If you'd follow Constable Henry into the bathroom, please, then we can address them."

The gray-and-white marble bathroom was spacious enough for a party of ten. The massive whirlpool tub could hold two adults comfortably. Laney quickly bolted an iron door against thoughts of Graham and Kristel sharing the tub. Sharing moments she'd been denied. Reese had always been particularly inventive in a bathtub.

Constable Henry set his briefcase on the austere marble countertop separating the his-and-hers sinks.

Laney eyed the case with suspicion as McBain cleared his throat to get their attention.

"Mrs. Dobson, you said a few minutes ago that you entered the bathroom only once to get a towel from this towel rack."

"That's right," she said, knowing intuitively that some ax was about to fall and it was going to come out of that blasted black briefcase.

"Did you open any drawers to look for first-aid supplies? Or wash your hands or anything?"

"No," Laney replied, wishing he'd just get on with it and deal his killing blow. She didn't even dare look at Ben for fear McBain would come up with a conspiracy theory. She thought about stopping the proceedings by invoking her right to consult with a lawyer before answering any more questions, but decided it would probably seal her guilt in McBain's eyes. She told herself that regardless of whatever evidence McBain had tucked away in that case, she had the truth on her side. "I grabbed the towel," she repeated firmly. "I washed my hands when you took me over to the neighbor's house."

"That's puzzling, because we found another red hair in the far sink and we lifted your prints off a bottle of perfume on the counter beside it. Henry, show her the bottle," McBain directed.

A bottle of perfume? Confusion clouded her thoughts as she examined the bagged bottle of Oscar de la Renta perfume. She owned a bottle herself, but it was at home. Or at least she thought it was. She didn't remember packing it. What's more, the sink was a good eight feet away from the towel bar. She didn't remember going anywhere near it, much less knocking something over on the counter that she could have inadvertently righted. She searched her mind for a plausible explanation.

Could it have been in her purse and had perhaps fallen onto the counter in her panic? How did it get in her purse, though? She rarely carried perfume in her purse. But she'd been so absentminded lately, maybe she'd done it without realizing it.

Laney jumped, startled by the boom of McBain's voice. "While you're coming up with an explanation for the perfume bottle, perhaps you can come up with an explanation for this woman's petite nightie we found in the hamper underneath the counter. We checked the tag. Quite a coincidence it comes from an exclusive lingerie store in Ottawa."

Laney reeled as Constable Henry supplied her with a plastic bag containing a wisp of lace-trimmed, royal-blue lingerie stained with blood. Her fingers tightened around the bag in instant recognition. Her eyes fluttered shut to shield her uncertainty. She'd worn the teddy only for Reese and certainly hadn't worn it since the avalanche. What was going on here? Was she losing her mind?

"Do you recognize the garment, Mrs. Dobson?" McBain asked her.

"Yes. I think it's mine," she said as steadily as she could manage, painfully aware the camera was recording her every word. Had she been foolish not to ask to have a lawyer present? "But I believe I have an explanation as to how it came to be here. My home was broken into a week ago. Not much was taken.

Money. My credit cards. But I noticed afterward a wedding photo was taken off my dresser and Josh was missing his favorite toy. The police seemed to think the thief was after drug money, but maybe the thief's real purpose was to steal things that could be used to incriminate me. Obviously someone knew Reese had invited me to meet him in Whistler.'' She spread her arms wide in appeal. ''Gee, I wonder who'd have the money to go to such lengths to set me up? Someone in the Butterfield family, perhaps?''

McBain and Constable Henry looked at her as if she'd suggested she had three heads and was descended from an alien culture.

''She's telling the truth,'' Ben cut in, exasperation evident in his throaty growl. ''Check with the Ottawa-Carleton police. Mrs. Dobson and her son were having dinner at my house with my son and my mother when the break-in occurred.''

''I certainly will check with the Ottawa-Carleton police,'' McBain assured him, fixing him with a challenging stare. ''How interesting that you're her alibi for the break-in.''

Laney sucked in her breath as Ben's expression turned to granite, the muscles in his neck standing out like sculpted cords. For a terrible second, she was afraid Ben would lunge at McBain.

But she should have known better. Ben always played fair and levelheaded, and always told his players on the Olympics that there was never any call for violence—on or off the ice. Pride blossomed with a honeyed feminine awareness deep within her when he tucked his hands in the front pockets of his slacks and met the corporal's stare with dignity glinting in his blue-black eyes. "With all due respect, Corporal," he said curtly, "I don't appreciate the implication in your last remark. Maybe you should try widening your view to look at the big picture."

Laney smothered a grin that was completely inappropriate for the seriousness of the situation and tried to squelch an insane desire to applaud Ben for being Ben.

McBain's beefy lips curled with smug satisfaction. "That's precisely what I'm leading up to...the big picture. If you'll both follow me back out onto the landing, I'll explain."

Laney lifted her chin and squared her shoulders, confident that no matter what McBain threw at them next, she and Ben could handle it.

Constable Henry turned on the massive crystal chandelier hanging in the upstairs hall as they gathered near the railing. Light refracted through the crystal prisms and glowed off the polished steps. Laney gazed in puzzlement at Corporal McBain.

"Look carefully at the top tier of the chandelier," he instructed. "Graham Walker was stabbed with a crystal rod taken from the fixture."

Laney gasped as McBain indicated a gap in the upper tier of the chandelier. Leaning over the rail, he removed the rod to the immediate right of the gap. The fixture swayed, its crystals clinking together with a melodic ripple. McBain handed her the rod.

Laney reluctantly took it. About twelve inches long, the rod was surprisingly heavy; its pointed, star-shaped tip was sharp against her thumb. Odd something so beautiful and simple could take a life.

"Go ahead, Mrs. Dobson," the corporal said, breaking into her sober thoughts. "Try replacing the rod on the hook."

Laney leaned over the rail. Even when she raised up on her tiptoes, her arm fell a foot short of the top tier.

"That's what I figured," the corporal murmured. "What are you—about five-two?"

"With my socks on," Laney replied, giddy relief washing through her. Surely this proved she had nothing to do with Reese's murder. Assuming Graham *was* Reese. But she had no doubt that the writing on both cards she'd received was Reese's.

Then she saw Constable Henry lift an upholstered bench that was tucked beneath a console on the opposite wall of the landing and set it alongside the railing. Laney bit down hard on lower lip and drew blood at the prospect of climbing onto that bench. McBain might as well slap the handcuffs around her wrists right now.

But the moment she climbed onto the bench, it became apparent the bench was too high. Though considerably taller now, her center of gravity was situated well above the railing, making it impossible for her to lean out over the stairwell without suffering a serious fall to the foyer below.

Laney felt like crowing until it dawned on her that the burly corporal didn't seem the least bit perturbed. After she'd safely dismounted the bench, he asked her for the rod and presented it to Ben.

"Okay, Mr. Forbes, it's your turn."

Laney felt her heart sink into a cold mire of dread. At six foot, Ben, of course, had no trouble slipping the rod onto the brass hook.

McBain was making it plain he thought they were in this together.

Chapter Nine

Ben swiveled to face McBain, his voice taut with impatience and concern that maybe, just maybe, McBain might charge them with murder and place them under arrest. "Nice theatrics, Corporal, but I had no reason to kill Graham Walker. All this proves is that his killer couldn't possibly have been Laney."

"Exactly," Laney chimed in, her eyes spitting blue sparks. "I hope you're planning to try this demonstration on Kristel and Nelson. They're both tall enough to reach the rod. And Kristel was home alone the night of the murder. Why aren't you questioning her alibi? She could have driven up here unnoticed. Maybe she detected a change in Graham's behavior that made her suspicious." Her hands balled into tight fists that she planted on her hips. "Or it could have been Nelson. Dallyn Vohringer hinted there was some animosity between them. Kristel and Nelson have been open about it, too. Kristel made a veiled comment last night that Nelson had expressed concerns Graham had married her for her money. And Nelson told us yesterday he thought Graham was too 'slick.'

I, for one, would dearly love to know where Nelson was early Sunday evening.''

''Actually, Mr. Butterfield was holed up in the penthouse suite of the Hotel Vancouver with his wife. The room-service staff have substantiated he was present.''

Ben didn't bother to hide his sarcasm. ''That's a convenient alibi for a man who can afford to pay others to do his dirty work.''

''Perhaps,'' Corporal McBain admitted, then pressed on relentlessly. ''But we talked to the person who delivered the food from the Chinese restaurant. Graham Walker was very much alive at 5:17 when the meal was delivered. That narrows the time of death down between 5:17 and 6:33 when the 911 call was logged. And you both were on the scene. So far, the concierge and the neighbors have substantiated your alibi, Mr. Forbes, but it hasn't escaped our notice that Mrs. Dobson may have found a way to entice her husband to remove the crystal rod for her. You said she had a towel in her hands when you found her. The murder weapon was wiped clean.''

Ben reached for Laney as she swayed like a sapling being battered by a gale-force wind, ripples of fear radiating in the pools of her eyes. For once he didn't give a damn what McBain thought of their relationship. He only knew Laney needed him. When push came to shove, he couldn't deny the fierce primal urge to protect her.

''And you think it makes a hell of a lot of sense for her to wipe the murder weapon clean of prints and leave her negligee and her perfume in the bathroom to incriminate her?'' Ben said forcefully, searching his mind for logical solutions. McBain might think he had staggering evidence against Laney, but Ben knew from years of working for the government that facts could be manipulated into many truths. And he had a lot more faith in the priceless woman he held in his arms, than in so-called ''facts'' delivered by the police lab.

McBain shrugged his shoulders. ''Your unexpected arrival may have prevented her from disposing of them.''

Ben's arm anchored gently around Laney's waist. A warm bond of strength seemed to join their bodies where they touched thigh to thigh, hip to hip, torso to torso. The softness of her breast was pliant against his ribs. ''Neither of us had anything to do with Graham Walker's murder,'' Ben said doggedly. ''Why would we?''

''Because Mrs. Dobson was afraid of losing her son and she turned to her lover to help her.''

''That's ridiculous. Laney and I aren't involved.''

''That's not what your neighbors say,'' McBain countered. ''The Ottawa RCMP have talked to several of your neighbors, who are willing to attest to the fact that Mr. Forbes and his son are frequent visitors to the Dobson home. And you, Mr. Forbes, recently spent the night there.''

Ben kept his arms defiantly around Laney and wished he had the right to do so forever. ''For crying out loud, Corporal. That was the night of the burglary. I slept on the couch because the kitchen door had been kicked in and Laney's son was scared. End of story. Next, you'll be suggesting we staged the accident last night.''

McBain didn't bat an eyelash. "Did you?"

"Of course not." Ben shook his head in frustration. "This is getting us nowhere. Why don't you give us a lie-detector test, Corporal? That will prove we're telling the truth."

"Yes," Laney agreed, instantly seconding his suggestion. "Then maybe you can get on with finding out who really killed Graham Walker."

"Now that's an offer I can't refuse," McBain replied, rubbing his angular jaw thoughtfully. "We'll set the tests up ASAP."

Ben just hoped they wouldn't ask him if he was in love with Laney. He'd have no other recourse but to tell the truth.

VINDICATION CAME that night for Laney at seven minutes after nine when McBain pronounced she and Ben had passed the polygraph test. It had been a grueling afternoon and evening. A polygraph operator had been dispatched from Vancouver and the three hour tests were administered in a room at the Fairways Hotel under a controlled environment. A camera mounted on a tripod was linked to a monitor in the room next door where McBain scrutinized the proceedings. Laney had been asked to go first.

When she'd finished, she'd spent three nervous hours in her hotel suite—while Ben was undergoing the test—drafting notes and questions she planned to ask McBain when their innocence was formally acknowledged.

She gave Ben a goofy smile—half-elated, half-relieved—and a stiff hug, and wished McBain weren't such an intimidating chaperone. The half hope that Ben might kiss her again stirred in her breast. Then she'd know if the intention behind that first kiss on the Seawalk had been friendly or romantic. Though maybe, she admitted to herself as she stepped away from Ben and the tantalizing scent of his aftershave, she was better off not knowing. Why spoil a perfectly good friendship?

She reached for the notes on the desk in the living area of their suite and focused on the events of the last few days. "Please sit down, Corporal," she said in her most businesslike manner. "I know it's late and you're working twenty-four hours a day on this case, but I have some questions and concerns which can't wait and may help you with the investigation. I'm not an expert on Graham Walker, but I do know Reese Dobson. If they're one and the same man, they must share a few traits in common."

"By all means, proceed, Mrs. Dobson," McBain responded, removing a small black notebook from the breast pocket of his patrol jacket as he eased his large frame onto the rustic overstuffed couch.

Laney checked her notes. "Assuming that Graham and Reese are the same person, the first thing that strikes me as odd is the money Graham Walker inherited from his grandmother. Kristel wasn't able to give us any details other than the grandmother's name—Millie Walker—and that she lived in Brandon, Manitoba. Surely this could be checked out? It seems to me Graham may have used or subconsciously tapped into Reese's knowledge and experience in the investments field to make a profit on the stock market. He may have used the story of an inheritance to explain his windfall.''

McBain nodded.

''Which brings me to the subject of Reese's electronic notebook. I wondered if you'd found one in Graham Walker's chalet, or in his office? Reese always carried one with him and called it his 'traveling secretary.' He was lost without it. Graham told Kristel he was going on a business trip. If Graham, like Reese, relied upon an electronic notebook to keep his life in order, then Graham must have had his notebook with him. If we could find it, it may indicate the name of a doctor who had been treating Graham for his amnesia. Or give us the name of a therapist who was helping him deal with his surfacing memories.''

Corporal McBain frowned. ''No electronic notebook has been found in the chalet, but if one exists, it may turn up as the investigation widens in scope.'' He cleared his throat. ''But perhaps I should clear up a point for you. Assuming Reese Dobson and Graham Walker are one and the same, we doubt very much that Reese Dobson ever had amnesia. We've run Graham Walker's social-insurance number and we've discovered it belongs to a Graham Walker who moved to the States over ten years ago. Graham Walker was originally from Brandon, Manitoba. But his grandmother's name was Tildy, not Millie.

''We've also checked the police reports for the avalanche. Reese was the last skier in a group of ten traversing the glacier that day. He was an experienced skier and could have rigged the accident, then skied down Mount Currie to Pemberton. The police report states there was falling snow that day. It could have concealed his tracks. For whatever reason, we believe Reese Dobson deliberately faked his death and took on another identity. We'll be delving more thoroughly into his employment with CDN Investments and into his business dealings with Connoisseur Specialty Wines.''

Laney gulped as McBain's information settled with a heavy and unalterable weight around her heart, confirming what she'd secretly been fearing all along.

Reese Dobson had abandoned his wife and son.

"I see," she said, studiously examining her list so Ben and the corporal couldn't see the hot tears smarting in her eyes.

"Laney, was Reese's electronic notebook returned to you with his personal belongings from the hotel after he disappeared?" she heard Ben ask.

"No." She blinked, her handwriting blurring on the page she held in her hands. She told herself that she was not responsible for Reese's choices. She'd been the best wife she knew how to be. And Josh was a great kid. All that mattered now was finding out the truth so she could close the book on this chapter of her life. "I assumed he had it with him when he was caught in the avalanche."

"So he may still have had it as Graham Walker," Ben pointed out. "And maybe he'd been using the information it contained to his advantage in the stock market. Or he was playing fast and loose with money

Kristel gave him and they made up the 'inheritance' tale to keep big brother at bay. Nelson may have found out about it though from Kristel's accountant. Heck, for all we know, Reese may have been involved in insider trading prior to his disappearance. Perhaps he grew worried the Ontario Securities Commission might launch an investigation into his activities and staged his own death.''

''But why would he contact me—especially after he'd married again? Reese was smart enough to know bigamy is a crime,'' Laney countered.

Ben shot a wary glance at the corporal. ''The only explanation I can come up with is that he missed Josh—and you. Maybe he discovered you were irreplaceable.''

Irreplaceable. Laney felt her body suffuse with a golden, soothing warmth, balmy as a late August breeze. For a moment she envied Rebecca Forbes, who was so irreplaceable her husband still longed for her four years after her death. Laney doubted Ben would ever love any of the string of women he dated as much as he had loved Rebecca.

McBain snapped his notebook closed and rose from the couch. ''I think we've already covered this ground. Unless there's anything else, I'll be on my way. I'll let you folks know what turns up. In the meantime, keep me informed of your whereabouts because you may be asked to submit to a lie detector test again.''

''Of course, Corporal.'' Laney gave him a half-hearted smile that hid the gnashing of her teeth and escorted him to the door. The tenacious corporal probably thought she and Ben would engage in wild, hot sex the minute he left. Not a bad fantasy, but it had no basis in reality.

"How nice to have the complete confidence of the police," she told Ben wryly as she returned to the seating area of their suite. He'd risen from the arm of the chair he'd perched on during their conversation with McBain and now stood on the area rug between the couch and the chair. Laney decided faded jeans had never looked so good on a man. The worn fabric cupped his taut buttocks and muscular thighs. She heard the rasp of the dark stubble shadowing his jaw as he stroked his chin with a distracted air.

"Hmm?" he murmured.

Laney firmly tucked all thoughts of slipping her arms around his broad back and slowly undoing the buttons of his denim shirt, into the "private fantasies" section of her brain.

But it took a moment for her to gather her wits and make her mouth cooperate with coherent speech. "What are you thinking about?" she asked, rubbing away a sudden patch of goose bumps on the backs of her arms.

Ben looked toward her, a sheepish smile that was oddly endearing, stamped on his handsome face. "Nelson Butterfield. The guy has millions and he's obviously protective of his sister. I'm just wondering if a sharp guy like him wouldn't have thoroughly checked out his new brother-in-law. Maybe he bought Graham's story for a while or he'd been keeping an eye on Kristel's bank accounts, then got suspicious and started digging deeper. He probably hired someone to tail Graham and check out his background. Let's say Nelson learns his brother-in-law has an alias, and a wife, and a kid. Nelson decides he's going to teach Graham a lesson for messing with his sister, so he pays someone to set you up for the murder. Hence the burglary and all the planted evidence.''

Laney flopped onto the couch and chewed her lower lip as she considered Ben's theory. ''It sounds plausible. But Nelson doesn't strike me as the kind of man who'd want to advertise the fact his sister had been married to a bigamist—especially when Nelson seems so concerned with Kristel's emotional stability. Why wouldn't he just arrange an accident to do away with Graham? He has the resources, and it would allow Kristel to save face.''

''Good point,'' Ben admitted. ''Kristel's the emotional sort. She might have done him in herself for what she perceived to be his betrayal of her. The guy *was* stabbed through the heart. Maybe she didn't have any idea who the other woman was. She just knew when she entered the house that her husband was obviously not on a business trip and was about to entertain a female companion.''

Laney sighed. ''Kristel definitely ranks up at the top of my list of suspects. I'm sure she isn't telling everything she knows. When McBain told me Reese planned his disappearance, it made me wonder how long he'd actually known Kristel. Not that I suppose it matters if he left me to be with her, but catching her in a lie might prove to the police Kristel isn't as innocent as she seems. I'd sure like to get another look at that photo on Graham's desk in his office.

Maybe there's a date on it or something. Or we'll see the outline of his electronic notebook in a pocket. I remember he wasn't wearing a ring or his favorite watch—'' She broke off suddenly. ''Oh, my God, that's it!''

Laney sat up taller, excitement coursing through her. ''In the photo he was wearing a cheap watch he'd bought the summer before he disappeared in Whistler! He'd gotten mugged in South America and knew he was going to Switzerland in the fall, so he'd bought an inexpensive watch to tide him over until his trip,'' she explained in a rush.

''Are you sure?''

''Well, I'll have to see the photo again to be one-hundred-percent certain.''

Ben grinned at her and Laney felt her private fantasies about him beat a path to the forefront of her mind at the devilish charisma of white teeth and dimples. She pressed her fingernails into her palms. Why couldn't Ben be old, flabby and have a receding hairline?

''Does your plan to see this photo include how we actually get into Graham's office?'' he asked. ''His partner kicked us out the last time we dropped by, remember?''

Laney waved away his concern. ''Details. Details. We'll ask nicely, beg if we have to, and make a fuss until he has no choice but to give in to our request so I can snatch the photo. Simple.''

Ben took two steps and stopped in front of her, amusement flashing in his heartbreaker eyes. ''Is that the secret of your success? It sounds like Scott's approach to getting what he wants.''

''Where do you think I learned it?''

Ben guffawed and Laney found herself laughing with him and enjoying the release.

''It's good to hear you laugh again,'' Ben said softly when their laughter had died away and she was trying to catch her breath. He brushed her shoulder with his fingertips; a platonic, casual touch between friends. There was nothing romantic about it except the starburst of awareness humming in her shoulder where his fingers made contact. ''I'm off to bed. We'll make an early start for Vancouver in the morning. I've got an address where we can exchange the rental car, okay?''

''Okay.'' She tilted her head back to look up at him and almost wished she hadn't. Her heart thumped and rattled against her ribs. The man was just too darned handsome for his own good.

''Good night, then. I'll call my mom from my room and check on the boys.''

''Good night, Ben.'' Impulsively, she reached out to grip his fingers and immediately regretted the impulse when she saw his sudden questioning frown. ''Thanks for being such a good friend,'' she stammered, quickly releasing him.

He shrugged. ''Hey, I owe you.''

Yeah, right. Laney watched him walk down the hall to his room, trying to close her ears to the whispery grazing of denim against denim that punctuated his every step and made her blood stir with awareness of the masculine power of his thighs. She groaned and sank deeper into the cushions of the couch. Friendship, she reminded herself sternly, was all she could ever reasonably hope to expect from Ben Forbes.

BEN GLARED AT THE MIRROR through bleary eyes and wondered how many minutes he'd actually slept last night. He sure as hell hadn't lost consciousness for more than an hour. He reached for his electric razor and derived a primal pleasure from the mechanical growl it made as he skimmed it over his jaw. Laney had clearly defined their relationship last night: friends.

For a split second there when she'd grabbed his fingers, he'd hoped she was reaching out for him. He'd searched her face for some encouraging sign to give him the courage to spill his guts. Thank God he hadn't! What a mistake that would have been. She'd have sent him packing on the first plane this morning.

And he wasn't leaving her alone. At least not until he got her safely back home to Ottawa and Josh.

"Face it, Forbes, your life is a mess," he muttered darkly. At least the boys were okay and safe with his mom.

But how he was going to get through the next few days—or the next week—sharing a hotel suite with Laney, he had no idea. He couldn't be in the same room with her without touching her. Sooner or later she'd begin to suspect how he felt about her. Hell, maybe she'd made that sudden declaration last night out of reaction to their all-too-brief kiss two nights ago.

Ben splashed water on his face and hoped a cup of

black coffee would improve his mood. At least they'd be driving the Sea to Sky highway in daylight. It would be easier to keep an eye out for trouble.

But the only trouble Ben experienced as they drove to Vancouver in the dented sedan was in making conversation. He'd never been so tongue-tied. So afraid of saying the wrong thing. It was a relief to arrive at the rental-car agency and deal with the practicalities of filling out the incident report and being issued a new car. Checking out the arrangement of the buttons on the dash of the replacement sedan gave him something harmless to talk about at every stoplight on the way to Connoisseur Specialty Wines.

Still, despite his resolve to keep his distance, he couldn't prevent himself from hustling around the car to open her door. Or protectively settling his hand on the small of her back for a fraction of a second as he ushered her inside the office building. Old habits died hard.

He even tried to open the door to Graham Walker's company for her, too. Tried, anyway. The etched-glass door was locked.

Laney knocked on the door. "Maybe Dallyn Vohringer closed up for today out of respect for Graham."

Ben peered through the glass, noticing the reception area was lit only by the natural sunlight streaming through the window. Then he noticed the empty display case and the empty space where the word processor had been on the receptionist's desk. The reception area had a vacated air. "*Cleared out* is more like it," Ben said.

"What do you mean?" Laney pressed her nose against the glass. "Oh, my God. Do you think he's skipped town?"

"Possibly. Either that, or the police did a search and seized everything. Let's try the office next door. Maybe they'll know what happened, or they'll let us use a phone to call McBain."

They were about to enter the neighboring dentist's office when a hostile voice stopped them in their tracks. "You have a lot of nerve. What are you doing in my husband's place of business?" Kristel demanded with cold fury, hugging a stack of empty cardboard boxes to her chest.

Ben had visions of a catfight erupting in the hallway as Laney squared off against Kristel. "We'd hoped to have a word with Dallyn Vohringer, but he's obviously not here." Laney went on to explain the vacated state of the office.

"Nonsense!" Kristel marched past them to the office door. "Of course Dallyn's here. He's expecting me. We have an appointment. He probably decided to give me a hand and packed up some of Graham's belongings on his own." Juggling the boxes with one arm, she rattled the knob, her eyes scanning the reception area as if she expected Dallyn to appear at any second.

He didn't.

"Do you have a key?" Ben asked.

Kristel dropped the boxes. They landed on the carpeted hallway with a soft thud. "Of course, I have a key." She dug into her purse, her face pale and pinched above the collar of her black turtleneck sweater. She wore a black wool blazer, matching slacks and high-heeled pumps. "I brought Graham's keys with me just in case. We'll just see what's going on. I talked to Dallyn yesterday on the phone. He specifically asked me to come at eleven." Kristel stuck the key in the lock.

A thorough search of the office indicated that everything was gone except the heavy pieces of furniture, the phone books and the company stationery. Nothing personal had been left behind in Graham's office. The photo on the desk had disappeared, as well.

"I can't believe Dallyn would take all Graham's things," Kristel murmured, grasping the edge of the desk for support. "Maybe the office was burgled."

Ben decided Kristel had led a far too sheltered life. "Thieves usually leave a mess and some sign of forced entry," he said dryly. "If the police didn't do this, I'd say Dallyn had a hand in Graham's murder and he left because he has something to hide. We should call McBain right away."

Kristel produced a cellular phone from her purse, but she insisted on trying Dallyn's home number before Ben contacted the police. There was no answer. Laney asked if Kristel could call the receptionist, but Kristel informed them that calling Bree would be redundant, since Dallyn and Bree were living together.

Ben felt his anxiety increase as he was patched through to McBain. McBain told him the police couldn't have already searched the office because they were waiting for the judge to sign the search warrant. Ben swore softly, seeing the chance of finding Graham's or Reese's killer slipping away from them. Dallyn could be anywhere by now. Had he done such a meticulous cleanup job to hide evidence? Or did he plan on setting up shop in another city?

"Wait a minute, I have an idea," he told McBain. "I heard Dallyn mention a warehouse when we were here the other day. Maybe we can find him there. He could clear out his office overnight, but it might take longer to empty a warehouse. Let's hope Dallyn isn't the type to walk away from tens of thousands of dollars' worth of wine."

Ben heard the rattle of papers over the line. "What warehouse?" McBain groused. "We don't have any information about an address for a warehouse belonging to the company."

"Hold on." Ben turned to Kristel. "Do you know where the warehouse is?"

"It's on the waterfront. I've never actually been there," she admitted. "Graham pointed out its general location to me once when we crossed over the Second Narrows Bridge. I think I know which street it's on, but I don't know the name." Determination lit her pale features. "I'm sure I could find the street if I drove over there. I don't want Graham's killer going unpunished."

"Good enough. We'll follow you," Ben said, noting Laney give Kristel's arm a faint squeeze. If Dallyn Vohringer had killed Graham, then Kristel was as much a victim as Laney.

Ben addressed McBain on the phone and told him they'd touch base as soon as they had a street name or a location. McBain said he'd have some men dispatched to the general area.

Ben and Laney followed Kristel's sinfully red sports car through the Gastown and Chinatown districts. She finally pulled over on Wall Street and parked her car. Ben parked behind her and helped Laney out of the new rental car.

Kristel gestured at the corrugated metal warehouses and dockyards lining the waterfront as they joined her on the sidewalk. The Burrard Inlet looked like a rumpled gray blanket beneath the cloudy sky. "I think it's somewhere around here," she said.

Ben squinted at the company names painted on the warehouses, most of them weathered by the sea air. Not a Connoisseur Specialty Wines sign in sight. There weren't too many people in sight, either. "Let's start knocking on doors," he suggested.

They split up, maintaining visual contact for safety. Laney and Kristel took the west side of the block, Ben took the east. Ben asked questions at four different places before he came upon a derelict tucked out of the salt-tanged wind in a niche between the wall of a building and a Dumpster. The elderly man in green khakis, mismatched running shoes and a stained navy raincoat unbuttoned over a tweed sports jacket, was curled up on a bed of yellowed newspapers, the neck of a plastic bottle sticking up from a scrunched brown-paper sack he held in his hand. The man opened his palm as Ben passed. His eyes were a dull, muddy brown; his beard, gray-streaked and sparse.

"Got any spare change, mister?" The man's arm trembled.

Ben dug in his pocket, knowing he shouldn't, that the old guy would probably buy more of whatever was in that bottle rather than a square meal, but he couldn't walk by and pretend he'd never seen him. He bent over and dropped ten dollars worth of coins in the old guy's hand. The old guy had been somebody's son. Was maybe somebody's father. The chapped, gnarled fingers curled around his shiny booty.

"Bless you," the man muttered.

Ben shook his head. "No, bless you." He crouched down to the old guy's eye level. The smell from the Dumpster was past ripe, but Ben had smelled worse at landfills. "This is a pretty good spot you got. You wouldn't happen to have noticed any crates of wine being delivered to a warehouse around here, would you? Maybe they throw stuff out—broken bottles you find in the garbage."

"Who wants to know?" the man asked suspiciously. He tucked his booty protectively in his pocket. "You police?"

"Who me? Nah. My hair's too long. I'm just making a delivery for a friend and I think I should have written down the address. I sure as heck don't see no Connoisseur Specialty Wines along this street."

"Con'seur, hey, hey." The man snorted and pointed down the block. "It's over thataway, son. There ain't no sign, but it's the dark green buildin' with the black stripe. The door's around back. But I wouldn't recommend you drink that 'spensive stuff.

I've had better-tasting vinegar. Give me a three-star sherry any day.''

''Thanks. You saved me a lot of trouble.'' Ben rose and slipped a twenty out of his wallet. The old guy's eyes widened as Ben held it out to him. ''Spend it on some food to go with the sherry, okay?''

''Hey, hey.'' The old guy burst into a creaky song as Ben jogged down the street to tell Laney and Kristel he'd located the warehouse.

He was relieved to see Laney and Kristel being moderately civil to each other. They called McBain on Kristel's cellular phone and advised him of the possible location. Together, the three of them skirted the green building to the door at the rear to await the police. There were no vehicles parked in the lot. And no windows to peer through to see if anyone was inside.

''How do we even know this is the right building?'' Laney whispered, when Ben tried the door marked Office and discovered it was locked. The wide delivery door was padlocked, as well.

''That wino probably sent us on a wild-goose chase,'' Kristel said, her mouth drawing into a tight frown. ''We could be wasting time.''

Ben stared at the lock, thinking. Had the old guy sensed a sucker and misled him? ''Let's try Graham's keys. Maybe one of them will fit.''

The fifth key he tried fit the office door and turned in the lock.

Ben opened the door partially, then paused.

''What are you waiting for?'' Kristel asked. ''Let's go.''

Ben looked at Laney and abruptly closed the door. "I don't think so," he replied. "Who knows what we'll find inside? Laney's already been set up once. This time we'll wait for the police and let them handle it."

Chapter Ten

The warehouse was deserted. Dallyn Vohringer had cleared it out, too, leaving behind a row of tables and chairs and a few empty cardboard boxes. In frustration, Ben kicked at a computer cable on the concrete floor. Vohringer's timely disappearance put Laney farther down on the list of suspects in Graham Walker's murder, but Ben would have felt a lot better if Dallyn was in police custody.

"Are you sure the door was locked, Ben?" Kristel asked as she surveyed the warehouse.

Ben stiffened. "Yeah, I'm sure. The key fit. You can try it yourself."

"This can't be the right place," Kristel insisted. "Wine must be stored under carefully controlled conditions and I don't see any evidence of those measures being employed. The temperature would fluctuate too greatly in a building like this."

"Maybe Dallyn took it all with him," Laney suggested, tucking her hands into the pockets of her jacket.

The RCMP constable from the Vancouver division, who seemed to be in charge, inserted himself into the conversation. "May I ask why you were at Connoisseur's offices this morning, Mrs. Walker?"

Laney clenched and unclenched her fingers in her jacket pockets as she listened to Kristel's tearful recital of how she'd made an appointment with Dallyn to collect her husband's belongings. The woman was a fine actress. She'd even earned Ben's sympathy. But Laney couldn't help wondering why Kristel was in such an all-fired rush to collect Graham's belongings? The man hadn't even been buried yet.

Come to think of it, Laney wondered if her husband's other wife hadn't been leading them around by the nose the whole time. But then, how could Kristel know they'd planned to visit Connoisseur Specialty Wines this morning?

"What about you and Mrs. Dobson?" the officer asked Ben and Laney.

Casting a glance at Kristel, Laney explained to the strapping blond officer that she'd wanted a second look at a photo on Graham's desk. "I thought the photo might prove Mrs. Walker wasn't being completely honest with the police and knew Reese before he'd faked his death. She may have even assisted him."

Kristel gasped. "How dare you insinuate such a thing! I met Graham in March."

Laney wheeled on her. "I'll dare anything to get to the truth so I can go home to my little boy and tell him what's become of his father." Laney told her about the watch she'd seen Graham wearing in the photo.

"That's your evidence? Graham owned several

watches.'' The condescending sarcasm in Kristel's voice gave Laney hackles. Laney *knew* the woman was lying through her pearly teeth and perfect lipstick. She just wished there was some way to prove it. Too late, Laney realized that even if the photo wasn't missing, the matching watch had been in her jewelry box and had been stolen during the burglary of her home.

To herself, she sounded like a bitter ex-wife. And jealous. And Laney didn't like the feeling one bit.

Yes, she'd see this situation right through to the end. Then she'd put it behind her and start looking to the future. Maybe date again. Perhaps marry again. She had no idea what the singles scene was like, but there had to be tons of men out there—equally as appealing as Ben—who'd make great stepdads for Josh. Before she knew it, she could be on a romantic Alaskan cruise herself, dancing the night away on the deck of the—

Laney smiled to herself as the name of the cruise ship she'd seen emblazoned on the life preserver in the photo of Graham and Kristel popped into her mind.

This was one little pertinent piece of information she could hardly wait to share privately with McBain.

McBain promised to check out the passenger lists for the cruise ship when they stopped by the RCMP detachment in Whistler on their way back to their hotel. He also informed them that they'd verified the warehouse on Wall Street was rented to Vohringer Imports and Exports. An APB had been issued for

Dallyn Vohringer, but they hadn't had any luck in tracking him down yet.

"However," McBain added, "we thought you might like to know we noticed something odd about the silverware we found on the dining-room table. It doesn't match any of the flatware found in the rest of the house. Mrs. Dobson seems fairly certain she didn't touch the silverware on the table, so on a hunch we sent someone up to Christine's. And bingo, it's from their restaurant."

Laney tried to assimilate what McBain was driving at. "Someone stole it from the restaurant after I left?"

McBain nodded. "That's what it looks like. It's possible your husband showed up for his lunch with you and left when he noticed this person. It also explains why he sent you a message via the young woman."

Laney felt the load of guilt she'd been carrying lessen somewhat. So Reese hadn't left specifically because of Ben. And judging by the romantic mood in the chalet when she'd arrived, Reese had been looking forward to their reunion. There was some comfort in that, at least. Though, who knew how much Reese had planned, and what the killer had contributed.

"So it couldn't have been Kristel," Ben said. "Reese would never have dared inviting Laney over to the chalet if he suspected Kristel was following him. But Reese might not have wanted to be seen by his business partner when he was supposed to be in Europe. Which leads us back to why Dallyn would want to kill Reese in the first place. Maybe the loan

Reese gave him came with a price Dallyn didn't want to pay anymore.''

The meeting ended with Laney feeling optimistic that the police were on a more realistic route to arresting Graham Walker's killer. The thought Dallyn might have gone so far as to break in to her home to set her up was creepy, but one she found more tolerable than being imprisoned for a crime she hadn't committed. For the first time in days, Laney slept deeply and awoke just before noon to the delicious smell of richly roasted coffee and cinnamon French toast.

Ben had ordered in room service for breakfast. Laney tightened the sash of her mint-green plush robe around her waist and tried to ignore the leaping flutter of her pulse when she entered the communal area of their suite and saw him at the table, his head bent over the sports page. His midnight hair was slightly damp, the ends curling at the back of his neck. He wore a blue sweatshirt and jeans.

A bout of longing hit her in the solar plexus. Laney pasted a confident smile on her face, told herself she was being ridiculous, and marched toward the table as if having breakfast with Ben was an everyday occurrence in her life. ''Hi, can anyone join the party?''

''Sure, it wouldn't be a party without you,'' Ben rejoined with a grin. An utterly adorable speck of powdered sugar clung to his chin. ''Sit down, I ordered plenty. I noticed you haven't been eating much lately.''

Sexy and considerate. Laney decided no single woman could resist the impact of Ben's smile when she was clothed in anything short of a suit of armor. Beneath the soft folds of her robe, she could feel her breasts grow heavy with golden heat.

"Looks like you're already throwing confetti," she said, playfully dabbing at the powder on his smooth-shaven jaw. But her teasing laughter died in her throat when her gaze locked with Ben's.

With a lightning-fast movement, he captured her hand, his fingers warm and strong around hers. "Hey, that's my breakfast," he declared.

Laney sucked in her breath as he drew her hand to his mouth and removed the speck of powder from her fingertip with a flick of his tongue. For a moment she forgot everything but the brief sensation of his tongue and its erotic aftershock on her body. Her legs wobbled. Ben released her hand and she plopped down in her chair before she made a fool of herself. Anyone could see he was just kidding around.

Laney helped herself to coffee and drizzled maple syrup over her French toast. With any luck at all, they'd be returning to Ottawa soon and this suite-sharing would end. She was just polishing off the bowl of fresh fruit Ben had ordered for her when the phone rang.

Ben passed it to her. It was McBain. His voice boomed a greeting over the line, then sobered. "The lab just phoned in the results of the comparison on the dental records. As I think we both anticipated, they've confirmed that Reese Dobson and Graham Walker were the same man. We'll hold the news to give you time to notify your little boy and other relatives, then we'll make it public."

"Thank you, Corporal." Laney glanced at Ben. "We'll head back on the first flight we can get, unless you have any objection."

She breathed a sigh of relief when McBain told her he had no objection, but to keep him apprised of her whereabouts in the event he needed to contact her. "Is there any other news regarding Dallyn Vohringer?" she asked.

"No, not yet. Could be he's holed up somewhere, but he'll surface, given time. By the way, Mrs. Walker confirmed that her husband kept an electronic notebook. It hasn't turned up yet, though. It's possible the killer took it. But the chalet will be thoroughly searched again today to make sure we haven't missed it."

Laney thanked the corporal and carefully hung up the phone, staring pensively at it. Reese had died four days ago. There was no more room for denials or putting things off. She felt Ben's hand settle on her shoulder and the compassionate weight of it brought comfort against the difficult task ahead. The time had come to tell Josh the truth about his father.

THEY MANAGED to get tickets on the first flight east Friday morning, deciding to make a slight detour to Toronto so they could talk to some of Reese's former co-workers at CDN Investments. Ottawa was an easy hour's flight away from Toronto. Laney figured she could be home in time to tuck Josh into bed, provided the weather cooperated.

But snow flurries delayed their landing in Toronto. They checked their luggage at the airport and took a taxi through slippery, clogged streets to CDN's offices in the heart of Canada's financial district. Reports of potential road closures sent workers hurrying home early. The modern, glass-walled towers on Bay Street—where just about every other building was a bank—resembled ice-cube trays in a winter wonderland. Laney much preferred the quaint clock tower and green copper spire of the Old City Hall at the end of the street.

Laney needn't have worried that Yale Sheridan wouldn't see her. Within minutes of asking, they were shown into the portfolio manager's corner office with its commanding view of the city under winter's siege. But all Yale Sheridan's attention was focused on the TV screens and masses of reports, newspapers and computer printouts stacked all over his office and on the floor, his razor-sharp, blue-green eyes giving the impression of missing nothing. The sense that every decision made in this room could result in profit or loss for the company's investors filled the air with palpable tension.

Laney had only met Sheridan on a few occasions, including Reese's memorial service, but she knew all about the legendary manager who kept CDN's investors in a state of financial bliss. Just shy of his fortieth birthday, Sheridan dealt with the pressure of being a star manager with a confident aura that could be downright intimidating. Though he rarely sported a tie with his tailored linen shirts, he had a fondness for suspenders. As he set aside a newspaper article he'd been reading and rose to greet them, she noted with amusement that his burgundy suspenders were patterned with the polar-bear design of the two-dollar coin.

Frank curiosity gleamed in his eyes as he extended his hand. "Laney, good to see you."

Laney introduced Ben and quickly got on with the reason for her visit. "I know the police have been to see you, so I won't go into unnecessary explanation. The long and the short of it is that dental records have positively confirmed Reese was the man who was murdered in the chalet in Whistler last Sunday. They believe he staged his death in the avalanche."

Sheridan bowed his head and rubbed the knuckle of his thumb against his brow as though contemplating the ramifications of her words. "I'm so sorry," he said after a pause. "How upsetting for you this must be. Has the news been publicly released yet? I haven't seen anything—"

"Not for a day or two. I have some family to notify first," she replied, trying not to think of Josh.

Sheridan paced a path through the paper maze on the floor. "I appreciate your keeping me up-to-date. I'll inform our PR department. We'll probably receive a few calls from the media once the news airs. Better to be prepared." He stopped pacing abruptly, his eyes pinpointing her. "As far as we're concerned, this is a police matter. Reese left our employ fourteen months ago."

Laney nodded. "I understand." Yale Sheridan's cautious stance was to be expected. CDN would do whatever it could to distance itself from the scandal that would result from Reese's bigamy and murder. But Sheridan didn't know all the facts. She took a deep breath for courage and plunged in. "Still, something must have precipitated Reese's decision to abandon his career and his family. I have reason to believe that he may have been involved in illegal trading activities in Vancouver using information he gained while under employment at this firm."

Sheridan frowned as though he was already feeling pressure from the firm's investors, wondering if something shady was going on at CDN. Not to mention the Ontario Securities Commission launching a full investigation. "Do you have any proof?"

Laney glanced at Ben and wondered if she should mention Reese's electronic notebook, then decided against it. "No. It's only speculation at this point."

"I can't speak for what Reese may or may not have done once he disappeared after the accident. Having changed his identity, he may have felt safe enough to take…certain risks. However, I may be able to provide some insight into why he may have decided to disappear at that particular time—and I mentioned this to the police. The fact of the matter is… Reese probably would have received his traveling papers had he not disappeared. He'd exercised some lousy judgment on a couple of recommendations and there just isn't room in this business for errors."

Shame stung Laney's cheeks. Had Reese suspected he was about to be fired and had run away from failing? Or had his work slipped because he was involved with Kristel in British Columbia? Laney's face grew hotter as she asked for permission to view Reese's personnel file so that she could double-check the dates of certain vacations he took. She wanted to know precisely how long Reese had been deceiving her.

"Say no more," Sheridan said with a compassionate nod. "My sister went through a similar phase when she found out her first husband was cheating on her. Once she knew all the details, she was able to move on. She's married to a great guy now. They just had twins." He reached for the phone and called Personnel to pull the file.

"You were quiet in there," Laney murmured to Ben out in the corridor, after Yale Sheridan had sent them on their way with instructions on how to get to the personnel department.

Laney felt Ben's blue-black gaze skim over her, from her toes to her nose, and felt a sharp response of awareness deep inside her when his gaze met hers square on. His eyes seemed to draw her in like a midnight-blue sky, fierce in its beauty, yet cloaked in secrets. Making her want to be party to his thoughts, a part of him. But he held her back from the muscled length of his body, his fingers digging into her upper arms. "Do you really need to know how long Reese was deceiving you?"

Laney couldn't tell if he meant to shake some sense into her or wrap his arms around her in pity. Not that she'd mind either one, as long as he continued to look at her like that. *Liar,* she told herself. She'd mind the pity.

"No," she said candidly, feeling a smile blossom on her lips. "That all seems like water under the bridge now. I just thought this might be another way to prove how long Reese may have known Kristel."

"Good. Just checking."

Ben's eyes narrowed and drifted down to settle on her lips. Laney drew in a sharp breath and froze as threads of desire twined a sensuous route through her body. Was he going to kiss her?

Oh, Lord. To her woe, she realized she wanted him to. Needed him to. Mistake or no, her lips parted as she anticipated his assault, blood thrumming in her ears.

But the *ding* of the elevator bell broke the spell. Ben released her and lunged for the door as though a rabid dog were on his heels. Laney let loose a ragged breath she hadn't realized she'd been holding, and finger-combed her hair with shaky fingers. Thanks heavens she'd be home alone in her own bed tonight, she thought, standing as far away from Ben's compelling presence as she could without looking impolite.

The elevator doors slid open on the sixteenth floor and she hurried out, eager to put some breathing space between her and Ben. A large manila envelope was waiting for them at the reception desk in personnel. Laney gave the receptionist the names of some of the analysts Reese had worked with during on-site inspections. Two were in the building.

They tracked Marv Shelton down in his office. The room reeked of cigarette smoke. He waved for them to enter, then pulled an overflowing ashtray from the bottom drawer of his metal filing cabinet and extracted a still-smoking cigarette.

His chair creaked as he leaned the full weight of his heavy frame into it. Laney gave him an abbreviated version of the facts of Reese's rise and return to the dead. "Yale Sheridan told me Reese may have disappeared because he was close to being fired."

"Let's put it this way, Laney, no disrespect intended," Marv said, punctuating his words with wild jabs of his cigarette. "Reese made a couple of poor decisions. He put his reputation on the line when he went against the advice of the team on Carmen Industries and Three Rivers and the investors paid heavily for it. He made Yale look bad and Yale doesn't hand out too many second chances. Some of our investors followed Yale here because of his ability to make savvy decisions. They might pull their investments if they thought Yale was losing his touch."

Pull their investments? Ben grew still as a theory slowly formed in his brain like a wooden puzzle being examined and assembled piece by piece. Suddenly, it didn't seem like such a good idea to be talking to Yale Sheridan's employees. He caught Laney's attention and glanced pointedly at his watch. "I think we'd better be on our way or we'll miss our flight."

Her delicate auburn-gold brows drew together, signaling her bewilderment, but she accepted the hint and rose. "Thanks for your help, Marv. Please give your wife my best wishes."

"You might want to call the airport first," Marv added helpfully. "I heard flights were being canceled because of the blizzard."

Laney was full of questions when Ben herded her out into the corridor.

"Shh!" he cautioned her. Cradling her face in his

palm, he whispered an explanation in her ear and felt her turn to marble. Ben tried not to think how vulnerable she seemed with her cold pale flesh and those wide blue eyes that had reflected far too much pain lately. What if Sheridan talked to the receptionist in personnel and learned Laney had asked to speak to other people?

Fear lodged deep in his belly and radiated out to his limbs. If Yale Sheridan had become suspicious of Reese's conveniently timed death and gone to such extreme lengths to set up Laney in order to deal with the threat Reese posed to the investment firm and Sheridan's reputation there was no telling what he might feel compelled to do to keep them from asking further questions. He was a brilliant strategist.

They couldn't get out of the building fast enough as far as Ben was concerned.

Even then, he kept a secure grip on Laney's hand and glanced over his shoulder every few seconds to make sure they weren't being followed.

Chapter Eleven

Ben tensed at the knock on the hotel-room door, then felt the muscles in his neck relax when he glanced through the peephole and saw a pimply-faced bell-boy with their room-service order.

He and Laney had entered and exited half a dozen hotels in an effort to lose any possible pursuers. When they'd stopped running long enough to call the airport from a pay phone, they'd learned their flight had been cancelled because of the snowstorm. They were stuck in Toronto for the night. Ben picked the best hotel in the city figuring they had top-notch security and made it clear when he registered that he wished his presence in the hotel to remain anonymous. He'd called McBain once they were safely in their room and he felt moderately better for having voiced his suspicions about Sheridan. But the corporal was three thousand miles away. And Ben sensed he was holding something back. Maybe McBain was just frustrated with the case, a feeling to which Ben could relate.

Ben knew he wouldn't feel at ease until the police had Reese's killer locked up. Laney would be back under her own roof tomorrow, out of his protection. The fear that something could go terribly wrong burrowed under Ben's skin and set his teeth on edge. And then there were the boys and his mom. What if they were dragged into this, too? Ben passed the bellboy a tip and wheeled the cart into the room himself, checking to make sure the door was bolted properly. There was no sign of anyone loitering in the hall.

"Find anything interesting?" Ben asked, stationing the cart near a table and two armchairs occupying a corner of the room. Laney was lying on her stomach on the bed, propped up on her elbows, studying the pages detailing Reese's vacation requests over the twelve years of his employment with CDN. A different kind of frustration reared in his groin as his gaze skimmed over her shapely legs and pert bottom, clothed in a second skin of Windsor-blue leggings. A matching lamb's-wool sweater shaped her full breasts and nipped at the curve of her waist.

Neither of them had luggage. The thought that they each might have to strip down and sleep in beds set three feet apart teased his imagination. She looked up, nearly catching him in the act of appraising the delights of her body. Ben glimpsed uncertainty swirling in her expressive eyes. So, she had found something interesting in those papers. Ben waited patiently, wanting her to know she could trust him with whatever she had found.

She bit her lip and Ben saw the imprint of her teeth on the sensitive skin. "I'm not sure. Maybe my doubts are making me paranoid or motherhood has fogged my memory, but I think Reese took several vacations I knew nothing about. Maybe he's known Kristel a lot longer than we think. Of course, some of these dates are years ago. Maybe I've just forgotten.''

Or Reese had cheated on her with other women. Hearing the forced breeziness of her tone when he knew she was hurting inside, Ben's fingers tightened on the stainless-steel dome covering her plate.

Emotions jammed in his throat. He set the lid aside and the smell of stir-fried chicken and vegetables filled their room. ''Maybe if you have something to eat, the food will stimulate your brain cells.''

''You're right.'' She clambered off the bed, graceful as a kitten, and Ben was aware of her every movement as she adjusted her sweater over her hips and helped him arrange the food on the table. He turned on the radio to a soft-rock station, hoping a bit of music would lighten the atmosphere.

It didn't. Some dumb song about a love gone miserably wrong.

Some encouragement.

As he cut into his steak, Ben noticed Laney was only pushing her food around on her plate. Ben felt tension clamp around his lungs as he watched her struggle to hide her feelings and battled his own painful need to offer her all the things a man was meant to offer a woman: love, comfort, protection, security and fidelity. She had enough to deal with right now without him unburdening himself.

Say something, make conversation, his mind urged. He talked about the boys and the hockey game they were playing tonight. "They should be home by now. I thought I'd call to see how they played. The Senators are tough to beat."

"Let me call," Laney insisted, jumping up from the table. "I need to talk to Josh anyway."

Her voice wavered and Ben stuck a chunk of steak in his mouth and chewed hard. Tears, damn it. She was on the brink of tears and trying hard to salvage her pride.

He chewed even harder as he listened to her talk to Josh, her voice falsely cheerful as she informed her son she'd be home tomorrow and had presents for him and Scott stowed in her luggage. Her back was to him, head down, her shoulders hunched in a dejected slump, but Ben could see the quivering of her fingers where she hugged herself around her waist. It was all he could do not to rip the phone out of the wall and tell her Reese wasn't worth this waste of her emotions.

Then, via the mirror over the dresser, he witnessed a glistening tear slide down the pale curve of her cheek. She hastily wiped it away with the tip of her finger. Ben choked down his mouthful of steak. Their gazes collided in the mirror when she hung up the phone. The look in her eyes hit him with the force of a sledgehammer: her misery, her shame, her self-doubts, her worries about Josh.

"Oh, God, Ben. Josh is never going to understand this…how can he—when I don't even understand?"

Ben's feelings detonated. Pain split his chest as he

bolted out of his chair. His fingers sunk into the softness of her lamb's-wool sweater as the first sob
wracked her body. He pulled her close, his fingers
splaying over her back, gently touching, gently re-
affirming that her body was made to nestle up
against his. There was no stopping his feelings now.
He pressed a protective kiss on the top of her head
and inhaled the scent of her silky auburn hair, filling
his senses and his heart with Laney.

He didn't want her to shed unhappy tears ever
again.

"There's nothing to understand, Laney," he whispered. "Reese didn't appreciate what he had...how
beautiful you are." Reverently, he traced the silken
warmth of her tear-stained cheek with his fingertips,
then with his lips.

"Or how beautiful you are in here." His hand
settled on her breast, over her heart. He nuzzled her
ear, reveling in the scent of her hair, in the delectable
softness of her skin. His pulse pounded through his
veins as she inclined her head toward the touch of
his lips.

Ben's breath grew ragged with restraint. "Or how
desirable you are..."

"Oh, Ben!"

Desire slammed into him as he hungrily sought
the softness of her lips.

Her sob turned to a sigh as she shifted and moved,
parting her lips to grant him access to the velvet
warmth of her tongue. She tasted of bliss, and magic,
and emotion, and Ben lost himself in the spell she
cast over him, in the questing thrust of their tongues

and the fiery need to touch and savor every inch of her.

He feathered his thumbs over her breasts and felt a surge of male pleasure when her nipples pebbled instantly.

"Touch me, please, Ben," Laney moaned.

"Where? Here?" he asked, sliding his hands underneath her sweater and cupping her lace-covered breasts in his palms. Her skin was like warmed satin, sinful in its luxurious texture.

"Yes, oh!" Her soft sigh registered in his brain as he released the front clasp of her bra and lovingly stroked the soft, creamy globes until the urge to claim her breasts with his mouth was so strong he had to break their fevered kiss.

Laney threaded her fingers through his hair, holding him as he pushed her sweater aside and growled deep in his throat as he devoted himself to worshipping each satin mound. The sweet taste of her pushed him deep into an abyss of ecstasy that he'd never known before. Filled the empty corners of his soul. He prayed this would be the first of a lifetime of loving between him and Laney. He swirled his tongue around a nipple as taut as a raspberry.

He felt Laney's fingers slide over his neck and dig into his shoulders. "Do you like that?" he asked huskily.

At her shuddering acquiescence, he chuckled and slid his hands down inside the waistband of her leggings. His body went painfully rigid as his palms molded the scrap of lace covering her smooth bottom. He ground his hips against hers, his heart soaring as if on feathered wings as she matched his movements.

Ben shifted his attention to laving her other breast as he slid one hand to the curve of her belly, exploring the dip of her belly button. Joy shot through him like wildfire as her fingers tentatively outlined the hardness of his erection through his jeans. His fingers lifted the elastic of her lacy panties and parted the silken patch of curls nestled between her legs. She inched her thighs apart for him and traced the broad tip of his maleness with her thumb. For a searing second, Ben thought he was going to climax right then like an inexperienced teen.

Struggling to maintain control, he dipped his finger in her moistness and stroked her, awed by her readiness for him. But she stiffened when he found the pearl of her femininity. Her eyes widened in alarm.

Ben's hand retreated to the lacy border of her panties and he kissed her brow. "I'd never hurt you, Laney. I want to touch you there, too." His voice deepened. "Most especially there. If you don't like it, I'll stop."

"Promise?"

At least there was no question she didn't want to make love with him. Her fiery hair spilled over her shoulders as she looked up at him. Ben's heart stilled at the trust in her still-damp eyes and he tumbled head over heels in love again.

"I promise," he croaked.

Her eyes sparkled like blue gems as he pulled off his jeans and underwear, first rescuing a foil packet from his wallet. Then he rolled her leggings and panties down her creamy thighs and tossed them on the floor near his clothes. Laney added her sweater to the pile and started work on the buttons of Ben's plaid shirt as he slid his hands over her hips. Having her naked and smiling before him was a dream come true and he didn't want to say or do anything to spoil the moment.

His desire nudged insistently against her belly as she slid the sleeves of his shirt off his arms. Ben ripped his white cotton thermal underwear over his head and flung it across the room.

Love and need twisted through him as Laney rose up on her toes and planted a kiss on the mat of hair covering his chest. The evocative feel of her lips on his bare skin raised goose bumps on his arms. Laney was right where she belonged. Ben closed his eyes and let his hands skim over her, as though verifying that all her delicious curves matched his fantasies. As her fingers curled possessively around his maleness, he found the pearl of her femininity, the core of her emotions.

He felt the tension build in her with every stroke until her response rose in a sensual song of pleasure in her throat.

Ben captured the sound with his mouth, sharing it, nurturing it with devouring kisses as his fingers stroked and caressed Laney. Satisfaction welled up inside him when he felt the first shudder of her orgasm ripple vibrantly through her body. Her song carried him so nearly to the edge, but they had a peak to reach together. He let her sing as long as he dared, wanting to give her as much pleasure as possible, then brought her quivering body down from its height and eased her onto the edge of the bed so he could reach for the foil packet.

He sheathed himself, fulfillment exploding in his heart and overflowing into his soul as he entered her and felt the tangible joining of their hearts. So close… Ben braced his arms on the bed on either side of Laney and thrust deeply into her again. Once, twice. Laney made a noise of pure contentment that mimicked Ben's thoughts. The heavenly perfection of her legs clasped around his hips. There was only him and Laney. Him and Laney. The rhythm whirled in his mind as her fluttering spasms embraced his maleness, coaxing him to share in her release. Ben couldn't hold back any longer. Arching into a final thrust, he reached the summit with her.

BEN WOKE UP at six-thirty the next morning, buoyant from the magic of the night before. The soft rise and fall of Laney's breathing brought a grin to his lips and a mercurial rush of hard desire to his groin. She lay curled up in a ball on the left side of the bed, defenseless against the world except for the sheet and thin blankets that covered her.

He stared at the tantalizing curve of her hip, wanting very much to inch closer and awaken her as she should be awakened: with warm kisses and assurances that she was loved. But he didn't have any more condoms with him and getting even a centimeter closer to Laney would be downright irresponsible. Especially when every single cell in his body ached to love her again.

Careful not to disturb her, he eased back the covers and reluctantly climbed out of the king-size bed. A cold shower and a layer of clothes and he'd feel safe enough to face Laney.

JUDGING BY the brightness of the ray of light sneaking through the crack in the closed drapes and the sound of the water running in the shower, Laney knew it must be morning, but she didn't want to open her eyes and put an end to the night before.

Ben had made love to her. Unexpectedly. Passionately. Thoroughly. Her body tingled and ached in places she'd forgotten a woman's body were supposed to tingle and ache.

Of course, it wasn't a dream. But it had been a mistake. A big one. She knew it from the moment Ben kissed her and told her she was beautiful. A cynical part of her recognized that his actions were probably motivated out of pity for her. But she couldn't stop herself from wanting to believe his husky words and wanting him to touch her. She'd needed Ben last night, needed someone to hold on to. A blush crept over her cheeks. Ben had filled that role, and then some.

The question was, how was she going to gracefully disentangle herself from the situation before a very nice friendship was irretrievably ruined? Ben hadn't exactly been spouting words of love last night. He'd told her himself he had a poor track record. His sexual relationships rarely lasted longer than three dates.

She briefly considered putting off her let's-be-friends speech until Ben's warranty expired, then ditched the idea as being too juvenile. She and Ben were both adults. They could handle this reasonably. Rationally. The shower shut off in the bathroom and Laney heard the muffled sound of Ben's humming. At least Ben was in a good mood this morning. Pulling the sheet off the bed, she wrapped it around herself toga-style and waited nervously for him.

A few minutes later, the bathroom door swung inward and Ben stepped into their room, fully dressed in the jeans and blue plaid shirt he'd worn yesterday, his tall form enveloped in a cloud of steam as though a fairy godmother had magically delivered him from a mystical place. Laney swallowed hard and felt a queer tightening in the pit of her stomach.

She clutched the sheet tighter around her, to protect herself from the disarming warmth blazing in his eyes. The blue-and-gray tones of his plaid shirt set his eyes off to devilish perfection. If he grinned, Laney knew she was done for and would probably do something foolish like drop the darn sheet. Only the thought that Josh might suffer for her foolishness kept the sheet clamped tightly to her bosom. Would she ever be able to look at Ben again without thinking about the way he'd touched her last night? About the things he'd whispered in her ear.

She held up her hand as he started to say something. ''No, me first.'' To her embarrassment, her voice squeaked.

Ben stopped and folded his arms over his chest.

"Thank you for last night," she went on, finding it frustratingly impossible to guess what he was thinking behind his neutral expression. "I needed a reminder that it's possible to have great sex with other men. But I don't want what happened last night to affect our friendship—or the boys' relationship. You're the best friend I've ever had and I don't want the fact that we've had sex to ruin that. There, I'm finished," she said with a lame smile. "Your turn."

Ben gazed down at the tousled silk of her hair and the flushed skin of her shoulders in disbelief. She actually thought he'd slept with her just to be nice! Hell, maybe he'd been similarly nice to other women in the past, but last night hadn't been about sex. He wanted to be with her *always*. To be a real father to Josh.

Ben clamped his jaw shut and debated his options. If he declared his feelings now, would she think he was just being *nice* again and doubt his sincerity? Maybe he was pushing things too fast and Laney was too upset over Reese's betrayal and his murder to even consider committing herself to another relationship.

Weighing his words carefully before he spoke, Ben touched the tiny indentation in Laney's small, pointed chin. "Nothing's changed since yesterday. You can always count on our friendship. I don't fly across the country for just anyone—only for Josh's mommy." The quicksilver flash of fear darting across her eyes at his touch and the slight trembling of her jaw confirmed his suspicions. She wasn't unaffected by their lovemaking last night. Just not ready. Well, he could respect that. And he could wait.

Last night had taught him that some things were well worth waiting for.

HOME. Laney stood in her own front hall and listened to the taxi drive Ben away. He'd spent most of their return flight to Ottawa trying to convince her that she and Josh should stay with him and Scott until the police figured out whether Dallyn Vohringer or Yale Sheridan was behind Reese's murder and made an arrest. Laney had thanked him for the offer of his guest room, and politely refused. It could take the police weeks, months, even a year or more to solve Reese's murder. Her office was in her home and she had a pile of work waiting for her.

And she'd flat out refused Ben's counteroffer to stay with her and Josh. It was the last thing she needed or wanted after they'd made love the night before. She'd never sleep knowing he was downstairs in her living room. She needed distance from Ben, not more confined intimacy. But she didn't tell Ben that. The explanation that her neighbors and the police—not to mention Josh—would surely take note of the event and blow the significance of it out of proportion provided a sufficient reasonable excuse.

Besides, she'd served as the fall guy in the murderer's game. She couldn't imagine the murderer risking exposure by trying to harm her now. Still, Ben had stubbornly insisted on entering the house with her and searching it for would-be intruders waiting to jump her. He'd even checked her phone line to make sure it was working. Then, after ordering her to lock the door after him and call him if she sensed anything the least bit suspicious, he'd finally taken his leave.

But when she closed her eyes, he was there. In her thoughts. The imprint of his lovemaking still present in her senses. Laney shook her head and groaned. She had far too much to do to waste time daydreaming about Ben. The boys were at a hockey game in a town forty minutes outside of Ottawa. Laney figured she had less than an hour and a half to herself before she had to pick Josh up at Ben's place. Hopefully, it was enough time to get some professional advice on how to break the news to Josh about his dad.

Laney carried her luggage upstairs to unpack and piled the gifts she'd bought for the boys in a fabric bag to take over to Ben's house. Then she made herself a cup of chamomile tea and called her friend Colombe.

The psychologist picked up the phone as Laney was leaving a message. "I thought you were another solicitor," Colombe said lightly. "So far today, I've been made a special offer on magazines, rug-cleaning services and gourmet chicken breasts."

Laney laughed. "Maybe you want to hang up. I'm calling to solicit your advice."

"Let her rip. I haven't heard from you in at least a week. I thought you must be busy because you weren't returning your e-mail or phone messages."

Laney's tea grew tepid as she launched into an abridged version of the last week.

Colombe offered her condolences. "Thank God you weren't arrested. What a traumatic experience for you. How are you coping? Wait, don't answer. I'm going to hop in my car. I'll be there in five minutes, provided it starts. I've been having trouble with the battery again."

"Please don't make a special trip over," Laney said before Colombe could hang up. "Although I'd love to see you, it's really not necessary and I have to pick up Josh at Scott's house shortly. I'm okay. I'm still in shock, but I'm optimistic the police will be arresting Reese's killer very shortly. I just called to hear your voice and hoped you might have some magic words of comfort I could offer Josh. It seems easier not to tell him at all, but there's a strong chance this will create a furor in the media."

"I agree you have to tell him. The only magic words are 'I'm sorry' and 'I understand.' At his age, Josh has very simplistic ideas about right and wrong, good guys and bad guys. He might wonder—or ask you—if Reese was killed because he was a bad person. Just be prepared to answer his questions and give him all the love and support you can. And remember, it takes a child—or anyone—time to come to terms with a loss…particularly when another issue is involved. Under the circumstances, it would be very normal for Josh to experience feelings of abandonment."

They talked for almost forty minutes longer, Laney skirting around Colombe's subtle and not-so-subtle prying about Ben. Laney had explained that Ben had accompanied her to Whistler and left it at that. She wasn't quite ready to share the news that she'd slept with him. It still felt too intensely private to share with anyone. The house felt lonely and far too silent as she hung up the phone.

She missed the boys and the sound of their video games. Laney glanced at the clock and gathered up her house keys and the bag of gifts she'd stowed by the door. Though she dreaded the task of telling Josh about Reese, she couldn't get to Ben's house soon enough.

"DAD'S A LIAR! I don't care what he did." Josh shouted, throwing his Spider-Man toy action figure across the living room. It knocked several leaves off her temperamental Dizygotheca plant, then slammed into a wall with a crack and slid to the floor.

Before she could stop him, Josh squirmed out of her arms, jumped off the couch and ran upstairs to his room, his feet thundering on the carpeted stairs.

Laney went after him. "Josh, honey, I know you're upset, but please come back and listen to me—"

"No!" The sound of his bedroom door slamming rattled the windows in the house.

Laney paused at the foot of the stairs and looked back at Spidey, who'd landed at a peculiar angle. She took a few seconds to retrieve him, glad to discover the toy action figure she'd bought to replace the one Reese had given Josh wasn't the worse for wear. Not that she was about to allow throwing in the house. Hugging Spidey to her chest, she mounted the stairs.

She knocked on Josh's door to announce her presence and tried the knob. The door wouldn't budge. Josh was pressing his full weight against it. But she could hear the sound of his sobs through the thickness of the wood.

Her eyes welled with tears and she pressed her hand to her mouth, resenting Reese for hurting Josh in this way. She prayed the emotional scars wouldn't last a lifetime. "Honey, let me in, please," she said softly.

She heard a muffled, "No."

Laney crouched down on her knees. "At least open the door a bit so I can give you Spidey."

"I don't want Spidey anymore. I don't want anything Dad gave me."

Laney's heart melted and her arms ached to hold him. "Oh Josh, I know this is confusing. This may seem hard to understand, but parents don't always act like adults, even though they are adults. Sometimes they make mistakes and do things that seem very selfish. I don't think your father purposefully meant to hurt you or us. And I honestly think he contacted me because he missed us. Missed you."

"So what? I'm glad he's dead. We don't need him anyway. I'd rather you married Ben."

Laney's chin dropped as she stared at the white-paneled door. Out of the mouths of babes. Where had that come from?

"You like Ben, don't you, Mom? You went away together."

"Josh, I'm not going to discuss this unless you open the door."

To her relief, Laney heard the sound of shuffling, then the door slowly opened and she saw a red-rimmed blue eye peering out at her distrustfully. She opened her arms and swallowed hard as Josh burrowed his warm, solid body into hers. She dropped a kiss on his blond head and smoothed his hair, hoping he'd forgotten his question. But he tilted his head back and looked up at her, innocence and hope blatant in his tear-streaked, freckled face.

"Do you love Ben, Mom?" he asked point-blank.

Did she love Ben? What a question! She felt many things for Ben, but was love one of them? Laney tried to puzzle out the intricacies of her feelings as she thought out an answer that would satisfy Josh.

"I'm sorry I didn't tell you the real reason I was going away. I didn't want to get your hopes up about your dad being alive. Ben came with me because he's a very good friend and he was worried about me." She took a deep breath. "I know how much you like Ben and I understand why you'd want him to be your dad. Ben cares about both of us because we're neighbors and you boys are friends, but he doesn't love me in the special way couples need to love each other to get married. You hang around Scott's house enough to know that Ben has other lady friends whom he dates in hopes he'll fall in love and marry one of them." She stroked Josh's silky hair. "Do you understand?"

"You could be one of Ben's lady friends if you

wanted,'' Josh insisted. ''I could ask Ben to ask you out on a date. I know he thinks you're pretty.''

Laney smiled as a rush of panic raced from her throat to her stomach over Josh's offer to play matchmaker. Just what Ben needed: more pressure to be nice to her.

''Oh, no you don't, honey. Love doesn't work that way. Remember when Scott told you that Amber Buckles liked you and wanted to be your girlfriend? You told me she was kind of pretty and okay for a girl, but you didn't like her enough to want to be her boyfriend. Then you wouldn't talk to her because you knew she liked you and that made you uncomfortable.''

Josh groaned, his nose wrinkling. ''Aw, Mom, that's kid stuff. This is different.''

She chucked him under the chin. ''No, it's not. When it comes to love, you let people decide who they want for themselves and don't interfere. Otherwise, you're going to get hurt. Now, get into your pajamas and brush your teeth and we can read one or two of those short mysteries from the book I brought you.''

''That's okay, Mom. I don't feel like reading. Scott and I stayed up late a lot talking while you were gone. I'll just go to bed.''

Laney felt his forehead. He didn't have a fever. Maybe this was just his way of saying he needed some private time to absorb what had happened.

''Okay, honey. I'll just wait till you're ready and tuck you in.''

She put Spidey on the foot of the bed while Josh

was in the bathroom brushing his teeth. When he came back in the room, he picked up the toy and dropped it in the trash can beneath his desk. Laney didn't say anything.

Neither did Josh.

She gave him a good long snuggle before she left the room.

HIS MOM just didn't understand. Josh felt the anger burning in his chest ease as he leaned over the side of his bed and reached underneath it for the plastic bag he'd hidden there when he'd unpacked his luggage earlier. There was just enough moonlight in his room to see. The plastic crinkled noisily and he slowed his movements so his mom wouldn't hear. Carefully, he removed the four wooden hearts: two big ones and two small ones. He fit the two big hearts together on his bed, then nested the two smaller hearts in the space where the two big hearts joined. Trying not to make any noise, he felt inside the bag for the photographs and the poem. There was a photo of each of them, him, Scott, Mom and Ben, all cut out around the edges so it was just a smiling person. Nothing to tell where or when the photo was taken.

Josh arranged the photos on the hearts, trying to figure out what Ben had meant to do with them before he'd thrown them in the trash can in his workshop where he and Scott had found it when they were scrounging for wood to build a city for Spidey and Superman to protect. It made sense that the big hearts were for Ben and his mom. The smaller hearts for him and Scott.

But what about the poem? It wouldn't fit on one heart. The piece of paper was too big. Josh read it and rolled his eyes. Gushy love-note stuff. He knew all about love notes. They made his mom cry and get all happy. When she was happy like that, she hugged people every five minutes and baked chocolate-chip cookies.

And Josh wanted her to be happy like that with Ben so they could live at Scott's house. Ben was cool. And he wouldn't leave them like his dad had.

Josh reached for a pair of scissors on the desk beside his bed. Maybe if he cut off the extra paper around the words, he could make the poem fit, too.

Somehow, he'd make it all fit. Once his mom saw this, *she'd* understand. Then they'd all be happy.

Chapter Twelve

Just when Laney thought she might be able to go to bed without giving Ben another thought, he landed on her doorstep. The unexpected knock on the door startled her, and sent her heart racing. She grasped the phone, ready to dial 911 as she stretched the cord down the hallway to peer through the fancy beveled-glass front door, which gave her a clear view of the man standing in a pool of light at the sunporch's French-door entrance.

Ben.

Her heart raced for another reason as she unlocked the front door, then let Ben into the sunporch, marveling at how he filled the tiny glass-walled room with his presence and his spicy scent. "I wasn't expecting you," she said uncertainly, drinking in the snug fit of his jeans, the brown suede jacket contouring his masculine, rugged bulk, the inky darkness of his hair and the ruddy patches of cold on his cheeks. If he kissed her, his nose and his cheeks would be cold, she thought distractedly.

A chill—or was it anticipation?—crept through the soles of her slippers and made her shiver.

"I tried calling first, but your line's been busy the last hour and a half."

"I was making a few calls…to my brother in Whitehorse and my mom's sister in Florida, and to a few friends I thought should know about Reese before the news is made public."

"How'd Josh handle the news?"

"He's hurt—and angry." She bit down on her lower lip, not wanting to mention the tail end of her discussion with Josh. Her grip turned slippery on the phone and she set it on the hall tree just inside the front door.

Ben followed her into the foyer. "Do you want me to talk to him…man to man?"

Laney's cheeks felt scalded. She wished some omnipotent force would bore a hole in her carpet and whisk her away from choosing between what was best for Josh and what could be downright embarrassing for her.

What if Josh bared his soul to Ben? Heaven help her if Ben pitied her enough to ask her out on a date, which, of course, she'd refuse. But she could see the situation becoming more and more hopelessly awkward. Oh, why had she slept with him? One covert look at him from beneath her lowered lashes gave her an honest answer to that question.

She'd just have to trust Ben to deal as he saw fit with whatever Josh said. "I'd be grateful if you talked to him. Josh looks up to you. But could you try to be subtle and impromptu about it? I don't want him to think I asked you to talk to him."

Ben grinned and a lock of inky hair shifted onto

his forehead. "No sweat. The boys have a practice Tuesday night. I'll look for an opportunity then."

Laney found herself thinking how natural it was for them to be discussing Josh's well-being together. She had to commend her son on his choice of surrogate father. "Is that why you came by, to see how Josh was doing?"

"Yes and no." Ben held up a yellow plastic bag, his expression sheepish.

"Did I accidentally pack something in your suitcase?"

"No. After you left with Josh, I ran out to buy a couple of cellular phones. I'll sleep better knowing we can reach each other any time of the day—or night." His eyes held hers for a moment, black pinpoints in blue fire. Laney pressed her damp palms together, battling his caring, and the insatiable ball of desire cradled in her core that flamed to life in his presence.

He held a phone out to her and showed her how to use it, his fingers sure, his voice patient as he explained. He even made her memorize the number of his cellular phone and made her promise to keep it within arm's reach wherever she went…inside and outside the house. Even in the bathroom or when she took out the trash. She wasn't to hesitate to call him if she heard a strange noise in the middle of the night.

Laney stared at him and promised. Not once in her whole life had anyone ever gone to such lengths to make her feel safe. Certainly not Reese. She was used to being incommunicado from him for days, sometimes weeks, at a time.

Ben's gift was downright practical, but in some inexplicable way Laney found it more touching than the jewels and silks and artwork Reese had given her over the years. Nothing she'd done to help Ben with Scott after Rebecca's death could equal Ben's show of concern for her and Josh.

Laney would almost have said it was romantic, except that Ben had never given her any indication he was romantically interested in her. Their lovemaking the other night had been elemental and primal. A pure and simple giving and sharing of need. He was a man. She was a woman. They were both under stress and needed a physical release.

It had been nothing like the lovemaking she'd shared with Reese, where the romantic atmosphere that most women dreamed about was perennially present: music, candles, flowers, mystery and lace. Reese had been a master of orchestrated seduction. He enjoyed the challenge of making sex a culmination of sensual stimuli.

There had been none of that with Ben. Only the two of them stripped bare, the touch of tongues and fingers, and murmured words of what felt exquisitely, wonderfully right. She wondered if the words Ben had said to her were real and unique unto her or if he'd uttered them to the other women he'd dated.

Laney trembled. Did she really want to know?

Ben unzipped his jacket, the metal rasp of the zipper shattering her thoughts. He tucked his cellular phone in the inside breast pocket and slid the zipper up, sealing the phone in the pocket of warmth surrounding his chest.

"Sleep well," he said huskily and slipped out the door to the sunporch.

Laney pressed her cellular phone to the hollow between her breasts. The porch door closed behind him with a bang as he disappeared into the cold winter's night.

Yet she felt him, close and warm next to her doubt-filled heart. Odd, what a strange bond a telephone could be.

LANEY PLANNED to spend a quiet Sunday with Josh. Taking care to tuck the cellular phone into her purse, she and Josh went to church. Then they stopped at their favorite pancake restaurant for brunch and shopped for groceries on the way home. Josh was short on smiles and conversation. He didn't mention Reese once. Or Ben.

Josh headed straight for his video games the moment he shed his winter coat, gloves, hat and boots. Laney called him back to help her carry the grocery bags to the kitchen table. Josh grumbled, but obeyed. At least that was typical behavior for him. Laney turned on the kettle for tea and hot chocolate, then puttered around putting the groceries away. The blinking red light on the answering machine signaled she'd received a few calls since she'd cleared the tape last night, but she ignored it. She'd deal with the messages later.

She had a mountain of laundry to tackle and, if she was lucky, she'd be able to induce Josh to play a game or two of chess with her. Or maybe he'd feel like skating on the Rideau Canal. Josh said *no* to both.

Laney let him be and went upstairs to her office, knowing he'd seek her out when he was ready.

The phone rang as she waded through the pile of mail on her desk, sorting out bills. *What next?* Laney wondered, as McBain boomed a gruff greeting in her ear. She closed the door to her office as they discussed his public statement identifying Reese as the murder victim in the Walker chalet in Whistler. There was no word yet on Dallyn Vohringer, but he had the RCMP in Toronto quietly investigating Yale Sheridan. ''I've saved the best news for last, Mrs. Dobson. We've received confirmation that a Graham Walker and Kristel Butterfield took an Alaskan cruise together the summer before your husband disappeared. Kristel's hired a lawyer and she isn't talking.''

Laney's breath escaped in a whoosh. Not that McBain's announcement came as any great surprise. But it didn't seem to matter all that much when or how Reese met Kristel or why he fell in love with her. She was more concerned with the here and now: Josh's emotional state, riding out the scandal Reese's actions had created—and her friendship with Ben.

Ben.

She'd felt him within easy reach all day long in the compact form of the black, high-tech cellular phone. Only sheer determination not to be more dependent on him than she already was had kept her from calling him thus far. Anticipation fluttered in her stomach. Now she had a legitimate reason to call him. To tell him the news...

There was a pause on the phone line. It took her a moment to realize McBain had probably asked her a question and was awaiting her response. Laney was mortified that she hadn't been paying attention. "Would you repeat that, please?"

"I said we found an electronic notebook in the chalet. And I'm catching a flight to Ottawa this afternoon in hopes you can identify it as belonging to your husband. It may be able to give us some answers if we can come up with the right password to access the information it contains. My flight doesn't get in until late tonight. Will you be able to see me tomorrow?"

"Yes, of course," she replied. "I work at home, but I've got some errands to run in the morning. Drop by any time after one—I'll be here."

Laney hung up quickly and reached for the cellular phone. Her fingers flew as she dialed Ben's number from memory. He answered it on the first ring.

Her knees turned to water when his husky voice caressed her ear, his concern blatantly evident. Laney gripped the edge of her desk and tried to disassociate Ben's voice from her memories of their lovemaking. It didn't work.

Perspiration beaded on her brow as images flooded her mind. Ben touching her. Thrusting into her. Need swelled and tightened in her throat. Laney stared at the little black phone. This was an unexpected downside to having Ben at her fingertips.

BEN RETURNED from a project meeting Monday morning to find Corporal McBain conspicuously waiting outside his office door. Unease trickled through Ben. "I'm surprised you made it past the security guard in the lobby,'' he said mildly, pulling his keys from his pocket to unlock his office door.

"A badge has its privileges,'' McBain said succinctly. "And so does working on a high-profile case. It's not every day I get to spend the taxpayers' money to fly across the country on a murder case. You should be honored by my visit.''

"Well, the same taxpayers pay me not to waste my time on social calls.'' Ben set his briefcase on the corner of his desk and closed the door to his office to give them some privacy. "Laney didn't mention you planned to make a side trip to my office....''

"That's because I didn't disclose my intention to her. There was something I wished to discuss with you privately.''

Ben's shoulders tensed. "I'm all ears,'' he replied, hanging up his jacket as McBain opened the briefcase he carried and removed a plastic bag containing an electronic notebook. "I take it that belonged to Reese.''

"We believe so, though we couldn't pick up any prints off it. We did find some business-expense files, which suggest it was Reese's, and a comprehensive list of golf courses and ski resorts all over the world. There was one secret file of interest that I wanted to show you. You see, I go into the memo mode and type in the secret password *L-A-N-E-Y* and this file appears.'' He passed the notebook to Ben.

Ben felt the hairs rise on the back of his neck. The message that had been written on the card Laney received on her wedding anniversary appeared on the display screen. Ben studied the electronic notebook and pressed a cursor key to scroll through the data display. "Is there anything else in the file?"

The valentine message flashed onto the screen followed by a memo to meet Laney at 5:30 p.m. Horstman Lane.

There were no more memos.

"Did you note the time of the meeting?" McBain asked. "In her statement, Mrs. Dobson said the woman told her to meet Reese at seven. The notebook clearly indicates the meeting was for five-thirty."

Ben handed the notebook back to McBain in disgust. "So you're relying on this over Laney's word? *Laney* isn't much of a secret password. Sounds like a setup to me. Reese was too smart to do something so obvious. Why would he need a memo to remind himself what time to meet his wife after a fourteen-month separation? I think he'd be able to remember that. Anyone could add a secret file if they knew what they were doing."

"Yes, I noticed you were quite proficient."

Ben ignored McBain's jab, which ranked right up there with the idiotic suggestion he and Laney had driven into a rock wall to throw suspicion off themselves. "I use one of these in my work, as do ninety percent of the people on this floor. I happen to know Nelson Butterfield uses one, too. The notebooks come with a thorough instruction manual. It's not rocket science. Did you find any other secret files?"

"No. Only the one. We haven't come up with any passwords as yet. But how do you know Butterfield uses an electronic notebook?"

''I saw him refer to it when he met Laney and me at the car dealership.''

McBain frowned.

''I'd be happy to take a few hours off to give you a ride over to Laney's so you can get her input,'' Ben offered. ''You're wasting your time here. And I don't want you wasting the taxpayers' money.''

McBain accepted Ben's invitation with a grin.

Ben started piling files into his briefcase. He'd only used up five vacation days going to British Columbia with Laney. He still had plenty of leave remaining to take a half day off. He could work at home later tonight. Besides, he needed to see Laney. Reassure himself she was okay. She hadn't wanted to see him last night when he'd called to tell her he'd just seen a clip on Graham Walker's murder—and his double identity—on the national news. At least it was a sketchy report that focused more on Graham Walker's marriage into the Butterfield family than Reese Dobson's life. There was no mention of his having a wife and son. Ben didn't know how long that would last.

But he was worried about Laney. He could hear her verbal retreat from him when she'd explained how totally unnecessary it would be for him to come over because she had the TV and radio off, the doors were locked and she was screening her calls. She and Josh were fine. Besides, he would see Josh on Tuesday night anyway for hockey practice.

Ben had the distinct impression she was more alarmed by the prospect of his dropping by for a few minutes, than of Reese's murderer suddenly showing up on her doorstep.

And he didn't know what to do about it. He knew she'd enjoyed every second of their lovemaking the other night, but he didn't have a clue as to what was going on in her heart. At least not yet. But he wouldn't find out anything more from a distance.

Women. Ben had no idea why they were so complicated.

LANEY FELT A SHIVER ripple through her and turned on the taps in the bathtub full blast, keeping her fingers under the stream of deliciously warm water tumbling in a waterfall into the luxurious double whirlpool tub. She'd felt a bone-chilling cold ever since she'd crawled out of bed this morning to get Josh ready for school.

She stared at her pensive reflection in the mirrors surrounding the tub as though examining her conscience for wrongdoing. She hadn't been sure whether or not to send Josh to school today, but he'd insisted, acted like it would be a punishment to stay home and dwell on his father's crimes.

She'd taken him to school and had a private talk with his teacher and the principal, filling them in on the situation. Then, she'd raced over to the university press's offices to pick up messages and a finished manuscript that was ready for editing. She'd bumped into Colombe at the University Center and spent a few minutes talking over coffee and bagels in the cafeteria, but even though she knew Colombe was more than willing to offer a listening ear, Laney couldn't talk to her about Ben. Everything was too unsettled.

Colombe, good friend that she was, had given her

a supportive, understanding smile and offered to come by Friday night with a decadent dessert and coffee after Josh was in bed. Laney gratefully accepted the invitation.

Maybe by Friday she'd be feeling better. Warmer, at least. The gleaming, dark-blue-and-white ceramic bathroom tiles, though bright and pretty, only made her feel colder. Maybe she'd picked up a bug on the plane. All that recirculated air.

Or maybe she simply dreaded McBain's visit later this afternoon. Maybe she didn't want to know whatever secrets Reese's electronic notebook held.

Laney scooped her favorite bath salts into the water. The water pounded into the tub as she stripped off her clothes and pinned up her hair. Then she realized she'd left the cellular phone downstairs in her purse. The idea of leaving the steamy bathroom to get it sent another chill through her, but she'd promised Ben. And the idea of breaking a promise she made to him bothered her more than the idea of racing through a poorly insulated house when she was already chilled.

Laney put on her robe and slippers and trudged downstairs to the kitchen. Her purse hung over one of the bleached-oak chairs. She grabbed it by the strap, not bothering to remove the phone. The sight of the unlocked front door as she made her way down the narrow front hall to the staircase made her glad she'd made the trip. Josh must have unlocked the door this morning and she hadn't noticed because they'd left via the kitchen door. He was always opening the darn door and traipsing out onto the sunporch to see how cold it really was, as if the thermometer reading in the minus degrees wasn't accurate enough.

She threw the dead bolt into place and hurried upstairs, depositing her purse alongside the pile of her clothes on the padded bench beside the tub in her haste to be out of her robe and slippers.

The tub was three-quarters full. She turned off the tap and lowered herself into the tub, sighing as the scented water covered her up to her chin. She rested her head against the bath pillow.

Heaven!

She could feel the heat sinking into her, sensuous with its embrace, unkinking the coiled threads of tension in her body and soothing the tangled confusion of her thoughts.

Laney closed her eyes. If only all of life's problems could be solved with a bath.

She wasn't sure when she became aware of the noise. It was a tiny creak. She opened her eyes and listened hard for what seemed like a full minute, then told herself she was being paranoid. It was only the house settling. Or the furnace. Or wind in the eaves.

Her eyelids drifted closed. She felt almost as drowsy and sated as she had after Ben had made love to her. Her breasts were full and heavy. Her limbs relaxed. The only thing missing was the muscle-plated hardness of Ben's body beside her.

As if by magic, the water lost its heat, no longer a suitable substitute for Ben.

Laney recognized a lost cause when she encountered one. Sitting up with a sigh, she turned the large, shiny chrome knob to let the water drain from the tub and reached for a towel. Out of the corner of her eye, she saw the bathroom door glide open soundlessly. Terror rose in her vocal cords as a draft of cool air bathed her shoulders and peppered her flesh with goose bumps.

Laney shrieked as Dallyn Vohringer stepped into her bathroom and closed the door, locking both of them inside.

"THIS THE STREET?" McBain asked Ben as they turned onto Laney's block.

"Yep," Ben replied. It made him nervous the way the corporal's eyes seemed to take in everything, making judgments that might affect Laney's life. His life. "My son and I live a couple of blocks away. Laney's house is the blue one halfway down the block. The one with the sunporch."

"Nice neighborhood. And I guess I'm not the only one who thinks so."

"Huh?" Ben said.

McBain pointed to a vehicle parked at the end of the block. "There's two men sitting in that gray sedan. Probably staking out their next job. Or Mrs. Dobson's house." Ben's blood ran cold as McBain's eyes narrowed. "I'll check it out just to be sure. Could be a couple of guys having lunch, with the engine running. Pull over here."

Ben did as he was instructed, monitoring McBain's progress to the sedan at the end of the block.

His breath froze in his lungs as he tried to move at a casual pace toward Laney's house. His boots made a muffled, crunching sound on the icy sidewalk. He hoped to hell McBain was wrong, but he had an uneasy feeling. Maybe he was just worried about Laney's reaction to his arrival.

Maybe he should call her and warn her he'd be landing on her doorstep in about thirty seconds. His worry turned to a tangible, living force when he punched in her number on the cellular phone and listened to one ring after another.

Why the hell wasn't she answering?

LANEY LUNGED for her purse and thanked God Josh was safely at school. Why hadn't she thought to lock the bathroom door? The locked door would have given her a few precious seconds to call for help.

Dallyn ripped her purse out of her wet hands. "That's a good idea," he said with a malevolent smile. "Beat me up with your purse."

Laney fell back into the slippery tub with a splash. She slid on her backside as her feet flew up in the air. "What do you want?" she gasped, trying to push herself up out of the draining water with her elbows.

"To tie up a loose end," he replied. "Namely, you." He caught her ankle in a viselike grip. His dark eyes had a brittle shine as he yanked her foot up, forcing her onto her back. Her free heel connected painfully with the six-inch-wide mouth of the decorative faucet as she tried to kick him. Laney yowled in pain, her cry turning into a gasp for air as her head plunged into the water. She kicked at him desperately with her free leg, the cruel pinch of his fingers on her trapped limb only enraging her further to fight. Josh was *not* going to lose her!

Water churned around her as she flailed her arms and fought to raise her head high enough to take another breath, her fingers slipping on the surface of the tub. Her free foot encountered a thick spray of hot water. Dallyn must have plugged the drain and turned the tap on.

Laney's fingers curled around the pillow in the wall of the tub above her head. Her stomach muscles cramped as she struggled to lift herself up and fling it at him, to buy herself a fraction of a second to take another breath.

Dallyn laughed and snapped his head around as a chirruping sound erupted from her purse.

Ben was calling her!

Anger and hope built to a white-hot inferno in her chest, but Laney could feel her legs losing their strength. Her fingers felt along the rim of the tub. There, something. Two gift-wrapped bars of seaweed soap Reese had bought her in Scotland. She grasped the bars, which were tied together with raffia, and threw.

They hit Dallyn square in the face. He reeled back and released her.

She heard him call her a nasty name as she scrambled to her knees and screamed, hoping one of the neighbors would hear. Dallyn clamped a hand over her mouth and shoved her head under the water.

LANEY WASN'T ANSWERING. Did that mean she wasn't home or she hadn't brought the phone with her? Ben jammed the phone back in his coat pocket. He'd progressed to Laney's front walk when he heard

three consecutive honks, then a shout drift up from
the end of the street. The gray sedan pulled away from
the curb, fishtailed as it made a rapid U-turn on the
slippery street, and raced toward Bank Street. McBain
followed on foot.

The sickening possibility that those three honks
were a signal of some kind sent Ben charging up Laney's front steps. He yanked open the door to her
sunporch, wondering why Laney had left it unlocked.
The front door was unlocked, as well.

The possibility that someone could be in the house
with her kept him from bellowing out her name. He
could hear water running upstairs. From her bathroom? Ben took the stairs cautiously, his heart pounding a drumbeat of fear that echoed in his ears. If anything had happened to Laney, he'd never forgive
himself.

He heard splashing sounds as he cleared the threshold into her bedroom. Had she decided to have a bath
and left her phone elsewhere in the house where she
couldn't hear it ring?

Ben tested the door to the bathroom. It was locked.
But a sharp voice laced with testosterone on the other
side of the door severed Ben's heart from his body.

''I'll teach you, you bitch—''

Ben recoiled a few steps, his gaze racing wildly
around Laney's bedroom for a weapon of some sort,
but nothing that looked capable of doing any damage
was within obvious sight. Ben put his shoulder to the
damn door. It gave way with a splintering crash and
smashed against the wall. A numbing horror pierced
Ben's soul as he registered the image of Dallyn Voh-

ringer leaning over the tub, holding Laney's head under water, her pale limbs jerking spasmodically above the surface of the water.

Vohringer whirled around at Ben's unexpected arrival, releasing Laney. With a flick of his wrist, a switchblade gleamed in his hand. Behind him, Laney bobbed up out of the tub like an ancient sea temptress, water streaming from her hair and body, and gulped for air.

The sound sent a shaft of relief coursing through Ben as he assumed a defensive stance and inched threateningly toward Vohringer, hoping to draw the man away from Laney until Corporal McBain showed up.

"Put the knife down, Vohringer. It's over."

"Not quite." Vohringer's eyes were hard and flat, his movements agile and confident. "I wanted to keep things nice and simple, but it looks like someone is going to have an awful cleanup job. You two are a liability I can no longer afford. You ask too many questions." He thrust toward Ben with the knife.

Ben heard Laney's cry of alarm as he evaded Vohringer's advance and circled slightly to the left, hoping to insert himself between Vohringer and Laney. Maybe if Vohringer had an unobstructed path to the door he'd choose to leave. Keeping his gaze trained on Vohringer, Ben used his peripheral vision to search the bathroom for potential weapons. Where the hell was McBain? Had he entered the house yet? And why didn't Laney have a plunger or a baseball bat in plain sight?

Ben raised his voice, hoping McBain could hear.

"What, Vohringer, are you getting rid of her because you failed at making her your scapegoat for Reese's murder?"

"You're so far from the truth it's almost laughable. I didn't have any reason to kill Reese. I had that thrill jockey right where I wanted him. All I had to do was show him the wedding portrait and his son's toy and he was ready to bow to my wishes. Just as you will bow to my wishes."

Did that mean Vohringer had planted Laney's things to cause trouble in Graham's marriage? Ben didn't have time to puzzle it out.

With an evil smile, Vohringer launched himself at Ben, the knife glinting dangerously as it whisked a fraction of an inch from Ben's abdomen. Ben grunted as he sidestepped the man's attack and landed a blow on Vohringer's shoulder with his elbow.

Vohringer wheeled around and came at him again, determination blazing in his eyes. Ben backed away, conscious that Laney was huddling in the tub to his right. Vohringer jabbed at him again. Out of the corner of his eye, Ben saw Laney move, saw a wave of water crash over the side of the tub and spill onto the floor. Vohringer slipped on the wet floor and lost his balance. Ben tried to knock the knife out of his hand and felt the sting of pain as the knife glanced off his ribs.

Ben planted a fist on Vohringer's jaw and wiped the triumphant smile off his face. Vohringer's head snapped back as the blow propelled him backward, his feet flying out from under him on the slick floor. His head hit the ceramic-tiled tub surround with an ominous thud. Something flickered in his dark eyes just before his lids slid down and his facial features relaxed. Ben kicked the knife out of the downed man's hand.

"Freeze. Don't move," McBain barked from the doorway, his gun drawn.

Ben nodded and doubled over, breathing hard, happy to oblige. "Can I at least pass Laney a towel?"

"Sure. Take her into the bedroom," McBain said, checking the wounded man's vital signs. "Then call for assistance."

Ben didn't care whether Vohringer was alive or dead. He passed McBain his cellular phone. "You call. I've got more important things to do." Ben grabbed a dry towel and wrapped it around Laney's naked body, relief and love bolting through him as their eyes met. She looked half-drowned and felt like a sodden feather pillow as he lifted her gently into his arms and carried her to the bed, where he sat down, cradling her in his lap. The enormity of what he'd almost lost descended upon him like a massive stone, causing his body to tremble and pain to radiate from his chest. That was just too damn close.

Laney's arms stole up and locked around his neck. The tightness of her grip brought a small measure of physical discomfort and a deeply satisfying smile to Ben's mouth. As did the warm, moist feel of her bottom against his thighs. He could spend the rest of his life holding her, devoting himself to making her happy and keeping her safe from life's problems. He smoothed the damp, tangled strands of hair away from her face, not the least bit concerned that his trousers and jacket were getting soaked. "It's okay. You're safe. It's all over now."

Laney nodded as Ben's reassuring words and the heat of his body slowly penetrated the cocoon of shock that cloaked her body. She couldn't even begin to tell him how thankful she was he'd saved her. How thankful she was to have him in her life. Vohringer could have killed him with that knife. She dug her fingers into the collar of his jacket and breathed in the rich, comforting smell of leather and Ben. The blade had come so close. Thank heavens he'd been wearing his jacket and it had offered some protection. She slid her fingers down over the damp suede covering his chest, reassuring herself that he was okay. Her fingers found a six-inch gash in the front of his jacket. Ben winced as she poked her fingers into the hole. When she pulled her hand away, her fingers were stained with blood. And so was her towel.

Laney leapt out of her stupor. "Oh, my God, Ben, you're hurt." She eased open his jacket and her mouth went dry. Ben's navy turtleneck was saturated with blood. Vohringer's aim had been far more lethal than she'd imagined.

She could hear McBain on the phone in the bathroom. "McBain," she barked over her shoulder as she yanked open a drawer to grab a handful of clean T-shirts to use as compresses. "Tell them we need a second ambulance. Hurry!"

TWENTY-SEVEN STITCHES. The thought of them in Ben's skin made the blood drain from Laney's face as she examined the gauze pressure dressing taped to his chest.

"Oh, Ben, you could have been killed," she whispered, gazing into his blue-black eyes and touching his chest, just above the rim of the bandage. The warmth of his skin seeped from her fingers and floated on a euphoric path through her bloodstream. "Promise me you won't show the boys your stitches. They'll be worried sick. I never should have dragged you into this."

His lean fingers grasped her hand and Laney gasped as the pad of his thumb stroked her palm. "I wanted to be dragged. I'd do anything to protect you. Don't you know that? Of course, it would be easier to protect you if you'd lock your doors."

"They were locked. I locked them before I went upstairs for my bath."

"Well, they were unlocked when I arrived."

"Oh, God, maybe Dallyn Vohringer found the spare key I keep hidden outside for Josh."

"It doesn't matter. It's over now." He tugged her wrist, the gurney he was sitting on in the emergency room squeaking as he pulled her closer until she stood between his thighs. Laney's heart stilled expectantly as he lifted her hand to his lips and pressed a heated kiss on her curled fingers.

He drew a long shuddering breath and gave her a sheepish grin that made Laney feel as if she were going to melt into a pool at his feet. Her heart seemed stuck between beats as he continued, "McBain is probably going to bust in on us any minute and spoil this, and I know a hospital emergency room isn't exactly romantic, but I have to tell you something and it can't wait any longer. I love you, Laney."

Laney stared at him. Had she heard right? He loved her romantically?

"No. You can't possibly mean what you're saying. It's just a result of everything that's happened." Laney knew she was babbling like an idiot, but she couldn't help herself. Ben was going to ruin everything and she had to stop him. "You've been looking out for me and Josh like a big brother...."

Laney's voice trailed off as he clasped her between the heat of his thighs, his fingers molding her pelvis into intimate contact with him.

Ben's voice deepened to a husky drawl. "I assure you my feelings for you aren't the least bit brotherly." The press of his arousal against her tummy substantiated his declaration. "I love you. I've been in love with you since Christmas. Remember when the kids baked the cookies and tied them to the balloons? That's when I fell in love with you. But the timing's never been right to ask you out. I had something special planned for Valentine's Day, but I discarded my plans when you told me about Reese's resurrection." His face flushed. "That's what I was working on that day you came to see me in the basement."

He was? What had he been working on?

Laney's curiosity was ignited, but she told herself it didn't matter what he'd been planning. The less she knew, the better. He was mistaking friendship for love...had felt sorry for her and Josh celebrating another Christmas alone...and she wasn't going to hurt

Josh by making the same mistake. Not when Josh had already been through so much.

It was difficult to think with Ben's warmth surrounding her, reminding her of all she might be giving up, but Laney had to put Josh's needs above her own. And it would be so easy to admit she loved Ben. To admit that he was there for her emotionally and physically in ways Reese never had been. But that was Ben being Ben. He was innately kind and considerate and supportive, always willing to lend a hand to anyone in a crisis. And she was definitely in crisis, standing in the emergency room, still shaking from nearly having been drowned, with damp hair and mismatched clothes. She had no reason to believe that Ben's feelings for her would be any more enduring than the feelings he had for the other women he'd dated. He hadn't exactly offered marriage.

She couldn't take the chance.

She swallowed hard. ''I'm very flattered, Ben, but I can't be more than friends with you. Josh loves you so much…he'd be terribly hurt if we dated and things didn't work out between us. As delightfully nice and handsome as you are, I just can't risk upsetting Josh like that. He's experienced enough loss.''

Laney wasn't prepared for the raw hurt she saw settle over Ben's features. A raw hurt that seemed to resonate through tiny receivers implanted in her body. His jaw stiffened as he asked, ''What makes you think things wouldn't work out between us?''

Laney closed her eyes as tears welled behind her eyelids. Why was he asking her this? Making her hurt him more. She bit down on her lower lip. Her heart told her Ben deserved an honest answer, but would he think she was criticizing him? Her chin quivered as she struggled to keep her composure. "I-it's no secret that every time things heat up between you and one of your girlfriends, you break up with her. You had three relationships last fall that I know of—and you were dating a librarian last summer. I'd prefer to remain friends with you. I need a friend like you a lot more than I need a short-term lover." Her mouth tweaked. "No matter how good you are in bed."

She felt his fingers brush her chin.

"Look at me," he commanded.

Ben swore softly as Laney opened her beautiful eyes and trickles of moisture seeped onto her cheeks. "But I never told any of those women that I loved them. I broke things off because there was no magic." Not like the magic that hummed in his fingertips as he fanned his fingers over the sensitive skin of her throat. Her pulse danced as though her blood raced for his touch alone. And yet he could sense her resistance, her battle to remain immune. For Josh's sake?

Or, because, in her heart, she didn't believe him? Didn't trust him?

He *had* dated a lot of women in the past four years. And Reese's infidelity had inevitably left emotional scars.

Ben was tempted to get down on his knees and declare his intention to wed her and love Josh as his own son, but the words couldn't get past the insidious inner voice that warned him if he did so she might only marry him for Josh's sake. She and Reese had

had a speedy wedding because Laney was pregnant with Reese's child. Ben wanted Laney in his arms freely, of her own choice. Not as a sacrifice for her son's happiness.

He spread his thighs, releasing her and let his hand drop to the gurney. "This isn't about Josh or Scott. This is about us. But you're right, all the magic in the world won't make a relationship work if the relationship isn't based on mutual love and trust. Tell me what's in your heart, Laney. Do you love me?"

An excruciating silence descended on Ben's ears, the silence perhaps an answer in itself. Laney's eyes seemed to plead for understanding from him, but he wanted to hear her answer from her lips.

Her lips moved, but whatever she was about to say was lost in the screech of metal rings as McBain slid the curtain surrounding the emergency-room compartment aside and interrupted them. Ben exhaled loudly and tried to control his temper as Laney took two hasty steps backward. The corporal's sense of timing was absolutely lousy.

THE REALIZATION that Laney might not love or trust him attacked Ben with the invasive force of a debilitating virus as McBain took their statements. Charges would be laid against Dallyn Vohringer when, and if, he recovered consciousness. He was currently undergoing tests.

Ben thought their behavior as they gave their statements must surely make McBain suspect he and Laney were being less than truthful about the details of what had occurred in the bathroom. Laney either looked straight through him as though he were invisible, or averted her eyes when he tried to meet her gaze.

Definitely a bad sign.

But he still wanted his answer. Even if it hurt.

Ben tried to pay attention to what McBain was saying about an APB that was out on the gray sedan parked on Laney's street. "It was a rental car. Vohringer rented it under an alias that matched fake ID we found in his wallet."

"There were two men in the car," Ben said. "Is it possible those two men were in the car that ran Laney and me off the highway?"

"Perhaps. If you're both up to it, I'd like to brainstorm a few passwords. We'll need solid evidence to put Vohringer away for Reese's murder."

"But Vohringer told us he didn't kill Reese." Ben frowned as he eased his left arm into the sleeve of his jacket. There was a sore spot in his arm from the tetanus shot the doctor had given him.

McBain gave him a patient look. "And you're going to take the word of someone who tried to kill you? Vohringer's hiding something, we just don't know what…yet."

"You and I can work together, Corporal," Laney said. "Ben needs to go home and rest."

Ben refused to be summarily dismissed. "I'm fine. Besides, I have no intention of leaving you alone until Vohringer's cohorts are behind bars. Josh can stay at my house tonight since he's with my mom anyway. We'll work out the details later," he said with iron in his tone when Laney started to object.

They sat around Laney's kitchen table for three hours eating pizza and making a list of the passwords they tried entering in Reese's electronic notebook— all without success. Ben was relieved when the corporal finally called a halt to the exercise and suggested a fresh start in the morning.

The tension packing the house seemed to escalate as Laney escorted the corporal to the front door. Mindful of his stitches, Ben rose from his chair and helped himself to a couple of extra-strength pain tablets from a bottle Laney had put on the counter. A little blood had oozed from the wound onto the old sweatshirt of Reese's Laney had loaned him, but the doctor had told him to expect this.

The thought that it was now or never made his footsteps heavy as he walked down the hall in search of Laney. She was throwing the bolt in the front door.

She must have heard his footsteps. Her eyes were wary as she turned around. "I'll pack some clothes for Josh and me. I think it would be better if I stayed at your house in the guest room than if you stayed here alone with me."

Ben put his arm out to stop her as she tried to slip past him to the stairs. "That's fine. But we have some unfinished business to discuss first. I asked you a question earlier and I want the truth. Do you love me?"

Her auburn head sagged against his arm. Ben's heart stopped. She made a tiny, unintelligible, strangled sound.

"What, sweetheart? I didn't hear you."

Laney tilted her head back. Her eyes were a brilliant, angry blue. "Yes," she hissed. "I love you, Ben. You're too perfect for your own good and I'm terrified you're going to break my heart and my son's heart. Are you happy now? You've forced me to admit it. I suppose you're going to ask me for a date next?"

"Maybe." Ben fought to keep the proud grin from inching across his face. Glory be, she loved him! But she didn't sound too happy about it. In fact, if he hadn't been injured, he was half-convinced she'd slug him. He clasped her face between his palms and saw the doubts and fears feeding the anger blazing in her eyes.

He touched his lips to the tip of her pert little nose. "So, Ms. Dobson, are you free some time next week to get married?"

He received a profound sense of happiness from watching her expression change from anger to disbelief to joy.

"Next week? Are you crazy?"

"Yes. I'm crazy about you. And I'm going to marry you, even if these stitches are going to interfere with our honeymoon." Ben bent his head to trace a trail of kisses from her jawline to her temple. Then he pulled back just enough to gauge her emotions from her eyes. He raised an eyebrow. "You're not suggesting a date. How's Friday afternoon sound? The boys have games on Saturday and Sunday. I don't want you or Josh to ever doubt how much I want to be a part of your lives."

Laney started to laugh, the sound as blissful and pure as wedding bells to Ben's ears. "Friday sounds perfect. But you're going to have to find someone else to coach the games. You'll be busy. With me." Her hands hooked around his neck. "Come here, Coach." The kiss she gave him filled him with magic.

THEY AWOKE THE BOYS in the morning and told them the news.

Josh shrieked and jumped down from the upper bunk bed in Scott's room to the lower one, where he promptly leapt on Scott. "I told you so, Scott," he crowed with obvious delight. "I told you they were in love. Now we'll be brothers."

"I'm the oldest," Scott declared, glancing out at Laney shyly from beneath Josh's torso.

Laney shared a look of amusement with Ben, who had his arm wrapped snugly around her waist. "You'll be the smallest, too, if Josh doesn't get off you," she remarked with a grin. Then she sobered as Josh let Scott up for air. "Are you okay with this, Scott? I promise not to be an evil stepmother."

Scott laughed as though this was an absurd idea. "Yeah, you make good pancakes and birthday cakes. And you're pretty for a girl. Where are we going to live?"

"I don't know," Ben said. "We're not sure yet. But we'll figure out something practical."

Scott gave Josh an elbow in the ribs. "You ask."

Josh rolled his eyes and looked sorely put upon. "Me and Scott want to know what to call you guys."

"Hmm," Laney murmured. "What do you want to call us?"

"*Mom* and *Dad* sound practical," Josh echoed.

"Well, then, Mom and Dad it is." Ben gave each of the boys a playful tap. "You boys hustle up and get ready for school."

Laney stopped Ben in the hallway to experience the stimulating delights of a good-morning kiss. Living with three practical men promised a never-ending supply of joys. Maybe as a wedding gift, the police would catch the two men working with Dallyn Vohringer and make her happiness complete.

LANEY GOT her wish when McBain called a few minutes later to confirm their appointment and told her the two men had been picked up last night. She hurried over to her own home to meet McBain, glad she didn't have to drag her mother-in-law-to-be along with her. Georgina had been so kind already with her time. And Ben had a meeting this morning with the Minister of the Environment that he couldn't postpone.

"You're glowing, Mrs. Dobson," McBain told her as he stepped into her narrow foyer and unzipped his coat. "I take it the news those two men have been arrested has lifted your spirits."

Laney blushed. "That, among other things. Ben asked me to marry him last night. We're going to tie the knot next week. I just got done booking the church and the minister."

McBain raised an eyebrow and smiled. "Ah. So you both finally noticed what was going on right under your noses. Congratulations. I hope you'll be very happy together. All the more reason for us to get this work out of the way so you can get your marriage off to a happy start and I can get the higher-ups off my back. Some influential corners are exerting a lot of pressure to make sure we have an airtight case against Graham Walker's killer.''

The corporal hung his coat on the hall tree. ''I checked with the hospital. Dallyn Vohringer has regained consciousness. He has a skull fracture. I'm hoping the doctor will allow me to see him later today. Those two men we picked up on the highway to Montreal haven't responded to questioning yet. But their names are Ivan Gillis and Rico Sanchez. Does either name ring a bell?''

Laney shook her head as they settled into chairs at the kitchen table and she poured coffee.

''They both have prior convictions for breaking and entering.''

''Do you think they're the ones who broke into my house?''

''It's looking that way. This turned up in one of their pockets.'' McBain opened his briefcase and passed her a plastic bag. Inside, though creased and torn, Laney recognized her wedding portrait. The one she was missing from her bedroom.

Finally, proof Dallyn had set her up for Reese's murder.

But they still didn't know why.

Systematically, they brainstormed passwords. Laney tried the titles and authors of some of Reese's favorite books. His favorite songs. The names of clubs he'd belonged to in secondary school. Names from his family tree. The names of the streets he'd lived on. Nothing.

She pulled out a reference volume from a shelf in the living room and they moved on to words associated with wines and the wine-making industry.

Then they tried words like *resurrection, double identity, secret identity.* "Try *thrill-seeker*," she told McBain, remembering something Dallyn had said yesterday afternoon when he'd tried to kill Ben.

"No match," McBain said with a sigh.

"Maybe it wasn't that exactly, but it was something like it. How about *sports enthusiast? Weekend warrior? Risk taker? Risky business?*"

McBain diligently punched away. "Sorry."

"I'll get a thesaurus and we'll look up synonyms for *thrill* and *risk*." Laney was halfway up the stairs to her office when Dallyn's precise expression popped into her mind. "Try *thrill jockey*," she called over the banister.

"Forget the thesaurus, Mrs. Dobson," McBain boomed back. "We hit pay dirt."

Laney ran into the kitchen and peered over McBain's shoulder. "It looks like a list of companies. Some of them sound familiar." A lump formed in her stomach. "They're companies Reese toured during on-site inspections for CDN Investments. But the dates listed are mostly within the last year. Maybe Dallyn found out about Reese's insider information and wanted in." She offered to print a hard copy of the list on the printer upstairs in her office. "Reese often printed off his expense reports, so I'm familiar with the process."

Studying the list on paper only increased Laney's certainty that Yale Sheridan would soon be sweating over the harm this list could potentially pose to the reputation of the firm.

McBain took several copies of the list over to the Ottawa RCMP headquarters to see what their experts could make of it.

Ben called as Laney was searching through the cupboards for a can of tuna to make herself a sandwich for lunch and planning to spend the afternoon line-editing the manuscript she'd picked up the day before. Laney decided she could happily get used to the idea of him calling her to discuss the details of their lives. She told him about the list she and McBain had found in the electronic notebook.

"That's great, sweetheart."

"Even better, the church is free Friday afternoon at 2:00 p.m."

Ben's voice deepened, rich and full of promises. "I'll be there. But first things first. I'm standing here in a jewelry store surrounded by diamond rings and—"

"Don't you dare buy my ring without me!" Laney squealed. "I wanted to do it together." She had to admit Ben didn't waste any time. She had no doubts whatsoever that he loved her. The thought of him selecting a ring to wear as a symbol of their commitment to each other was thrilling, too.

Ben laughed. "That's what I thought. Why don't you meet me and we'll have lunch and make a special occasion of it?"

Laney made an executive decision to abandon the tuna and the manuscript. She could read it tonight while Josh was at hockey practice, and finish it later after Josh had gone to bed. She probably wouldn't be able to sleep, anyway. It would give her something productive to do. She'd already told Ben that they were not going to sleep together until after the wedding. Despite Ben's denials, she was certain sex was on the list of forbidden heavy-duty activities the doctor had recommended he avoid to prevent tearing his stitches.

She was barreling out of the house, feeling like the sexiest woman alive in a soft, clinging outfit, with dabs of perfume placed in strategic spots for Ben, when a car pulled up in her driveway, blocking her in.

"Laney, thank heavens!" her friend Colombe cried, scrambling out of her canary-yellow BMW. "I've been worried sick about you. I'm tired of reaching your voice mail. How is Josh? How did he take the news?"

Laney hugged her tall friend. "I'm sorry, Colombe. Everything's been so crazy, I've just been ignoring the phone. But I'm wonderful. Josh is doing okay. And I'm getting married!"

"Married! To Ben?"

Laney laughed at the shock on her friend's face. Then the concern. "I know. I know. It's sudden. But he asked me last night and I'm going off to meet him right now to buy the rings. Our rings. It sounds so wonderful, doesn't it? I thought I loved Reese, but this feeling with Ben is so—" Laney spread her arms wide and twirled around, slipping a bit on the icy sidewalk. "Encompassing. Does that make sense?"

"I guess so, Laney, but—"

Laney wasn't in the mood to hear words of advice. She'd been mourning life and missed opportunities since Reese's initial disappearance. Now she wanted to live it up. She blithely gripped Colombe's arms and cut her off. "Listen, what are you doing next Friday afternoon? Ben and I are getting married and I want you to be my Matron of Honor. Or is *Best Woman* the politically correct term now?"

"Does this mean we get to go shopping together for dresses?" Colombe asked.

"Yes," Laney stated emphatically.

"Then I accept. Though you realize we're going to look like a giraffe standing next to a mouse at the altar."

Laney flicked her wrist at her cluttered, yet adorable Victorian cottage. "As if I cared about aesthetics. Not to worry. The wedding promises to be a zoo anyway."

Colombe choked back a laugh and hugged Laney again. "I wouldn't miss it for the world."

THE RESOURCES of the RCMP were swift and sure in determining the meaning of the list of companies and dates. By the end of the week, McBain called to inform them that the companies were indeed businesses that Reese had toured in the course of his job at CDN Investments. The dates coincided with reported burglaries, in which the computer systems of the businesses had been stolen. The police suspected that Reese and Dallyn's import/export wine business was a front for a criminal ring selling information technology to foreign countries.

Laney sighed. At least they knew the truth now. And Yale Sheridan was probably relieved the authorities wouldn't soon be breathing down his neck.

"That explains the lack of equipment in the warehouse and the wino's comment about the wine tasting like vinegar. I should have clued in to that before," she heard Ben tell McBain from the extension in his bedroom. Laney was listening in on the kitchen extension in Ben's house.

"But why did Vohringer leave Reese's electronic notebook in the chalet—especially when it had the potential to give away his operation?" Laney asked.

"I think you showed up at the house before he could find it. We found it in a boot in the downstairs closet. We're not sure how it got there. Maybe it fell out of his coat. But it also explains why he tried to kill you. He planned to make you the fall guy for this scheme, but when you weren't the patsy he expected and you kept pushing for the truth, he realized you posed a serious threat. Kristel didn't know anything about Reese's previous employment as a financial analyst, but you knew enough to start putting pieces together."

Which explained what Dallyn had meant when he'd told her that she and Ben were a liability and asked too many questions.

Laney wound a lock of hair around her finger and gazed at the piles of craft materials, cans of gold spray paint and tulle littering the kitchen table. Georgina was fashioning centerpieces and napkin rings for the small reception, which would be held at one of Laney's favorite restaurants. They were exquisite, with a moon, sun and stars motif, because Ben had told her he'd fallen in love with her when they'd stood with the boys and watched their Christmas balloons disappear into a starry sky. "But that doesn't explain Reese's memo for me to meet him at five-thirty. The girl definitely said seven."

Ben chipped in a theory. "Maybe Reese's memo meant he planned to be back at the house by five-thirty to prepare for your arrival."

"I suppose," Laney agreed. She hung up the phone feeling somewhat overwhelmed. Maybe it was from finally learning what Reese was up to. Or maybe it was a case of cold feet and the pressure of knowing the wedding was only a week away. She must be crazy in love with Ben to think she could pull this off. She picked up a shiny gold star that had escaped from the table and landed on the floor. Laney balanced it on the tip of her index finger. Oh, yes, she was crazy in love, all right. Somehow. Some way. It helped having a crafty mother-in-law, who deserved a restful week away as a treat for being such an angel with the boys and the wedding plans. Laney sighed. Maybe after she and Ben said their vows, this queasy feeling would go away.

"HERE, MOM, we have a present for you," Josh and Scott said in unison as the door to the room reserved for brides in the church opened.

Laney turned away from the mirror and smiled with pride at her two little men in navy suits, faces bright and hair slightly ruffled, sharing the weight of a silver-wrapped package between them. She hoped whatever was in the box wasn't fragile. "Oh, did someone give you a gift? Go give it to Uncle Rob and ask him to lock it in the trunk of his car."

"No, Mom," Josh said, as Laney straightened the calla lily trimmed with a gold moon that was pinned to his lapel. The boys were going to walk her down the aisle. "You don't understand. This is a present for you from me and Scott. You have to open it now."

"Yeah, Mom," Scott agreed, ducking his head before Laney could correct an unruly cowlick on his crown. "It's your something old, something new, something borrowed and something blue. Grandma said a bride has to have all that stuff for good luck."

"Well, you certainly want good luck don't you, Laney?" Colombe quipped, succeeding where Laney had failed and smoothing down Scott's cowlick with Laney's hairbrush.

"You boys are my good luck. But I was never one to turn down a present." Laney held out her hands for the box. Its weight made her wonder immediately how she was ever going to wear whatever was inside. She hoped Grandma had explained that to the boys.

Laney set the box beside her beribboned bride's bouquet on the table and tore off the heavy silver paper the boys had decorated with gold stars. "Oh, my goodness," she breathed when she lifted the lid of the box and saw four familiar faces beaming up at her from four connecting hearts. There was also a poem. The oak wood had been beautifully stained, the perimeter painted with blue hearts and the whole thing varnished. Was this the valentine Ben had told her about? "This is beautiful, boys. But how did you get this?"

"We found it in Dad's workshop and we finished it for him. See, it's a puzzle, Mom," Josh explained. "The four of us fit together like a family. Ben made it and wrote the poem. It's gushy."

Laney let the "found" reference go. She could talk to the boys about snooping through the trash later. Tears sprang to her eyes as she read Ben's poem:

> To Laney,
> My friend you are and will always be
> Your warmth and smile light up our lives
> Your laughter brings us joy
> And draws us close in love and harmony.
> I'm offering you dinner and a fine wine.
> If only you'll be my Valentine.
> Affectionately, Ben

Scott tugged on Laney's arm. "Why are you crying, Mom? Don't you like it? I painted on the blue hearts 'cause Grandma said we needed something blue. The photos are old, the puzzle is new, and the varnish we borrowed from Grandma. She helped us do it."

Laney nodded, too choked-up to speak, and wiped her cheeks with her fingers. She was probably ruining her makeup.

"Of course she likes it," Josh explained patiently. "She always cries when she gets good presents. When she starts talking a lot it usually means she doesn't like it."

Laney caught both boys in a tight hug. "I love it. Thank you." Since they were trapped in her arms without means of escape, she risked kissing each of her sons on the cheek. "Would you please take it outside and ask Grandma to put it someplace near the front of the church where everyone can see it? The guests should be arriving now, so you need to usher them into the pews. The minister will tell you when it's time to walk me down the aisle."

Organ music filled the little room as the boys filed out, taking great care of the heart in their charge.

"I must look a mess," Laney said, turning to Colombe with a sigh of contentment. "All that primping down the drain."

"You look happier than any woman has a right to be," Colombe replied, suddenly brusque. "Sit here and I'll fix your makeup. Your tears have left tracks." Laney obediently sat down in front of the mirror, allowing Colombe to touch up the damaged spots. Her heart hammered with anticipation to see Ben in his navy suit, waiting for her at the end of the aisle. Tuxes, she'd learned from Ben, were very impractical.

Colombe's voice drifted into the pink glow of her thoughts. "You realize how unbelievably lucky you are to be marrying again after being jilted so badly. I suppose you and Ben will have more babies. I can picture you with a little girl with curly auburn hair to drive Scott and Josh nuts."

Laney heard something in Colombe's tone she'd never heard before...envy...a hint of bitterness. Colombe had confided once that she and her husband had discovered she couldn't bear children.

In a rush of sympathy, Laney laid her hand on Colombe's wrist. She looked stunning in the royal-blue sheath dress, her silver hair pulled up in a sophisticated knot. And she'd substituted contact lenses for the glasses she normally wore. "I know happiness will find its way to you—just as it did to me."

Colombe shook her head and moved to the table beside the door where she picked up Laney's wedding bouquet. Her back was to Laney, but Laney could see the long streamers trailing from the cluster of white calla lilies flowing over her fingers as she made a minute adjustment to the arrangement. "At least," she said, finally turning around and raising her eyes to meet Laney's gaze, "I received some satisfaction from knowing that Kristel was suffering the same misery I'd suffered. How did it feel, Laney, to know you'd been replaced by someone younger and prettier and wealthier?"

Laney stared at Colombe in mute shock. What was she saying?

Colombe took a step closer to Laney, the knuckles of her fingers white against the white streamers of the bouquet. "Did you feel humiliated? Did you hate knowing your husband had shared sacred vows with someone else? Shared his body?" Colombe laughed very softly. Hollowly. "Perhaps, little innocent Laney, you don't want to know how thriftily he sent copies of the same poem to each wife. Such a pity Kristel hadn't been pregnant, so you'd feel the pain of knowing another woman bore your husband's child.''

Laney steeled herself against the spiteful words Colombe was torturing her with. She forced her lungs to operate, forced her throat to produce words. ''Y-you were married to Reese, too?''

''Yes. Only he wasn't Reese Dobson. His real name was Patrick Cyr. He supposedly drowned one day in a sailing mishap in Halifax six months before Reese Dobson supposedly died in an avalanche. Patrick's body was never found.'' Colombe wrenched a lily out of the bouquet and threw it to the ground. ''I didn't know he was leading a double life until I'd found the love poems addressed to you and Kristel Walker in a hidey-hole in our house when I had a closet wall torn down for renovations. I don't know which propelled me most, anger or curiosity. But I had to meet you both. I was amazed that your husband had also died, but when I got to Vancouver and saw Graham Walker, I knew why. And I decided someone was going to make him pay.''

Laney straightened. ''So you took your sabbatical here to set me up. Became my friend. Took my lingerie. Some hairs from my brush. And the silverware from the restaurant. Did Reese even send for me? Or was that you, too?''

''That was me. I called him in Vancouver. That shook him up. We arranged a secret rendezvous in Whistler for Valentine's Day. I think somehow he thought he could pacify me into keeping his secret with the flowers and the candles and the meal. I rather enjoyed the idea of his rich, pretty wife pining away for him while he was with me. And, of course, there you were, the mother of his child, alone in a restaurant, stood up on Valentine's Day. There seemed a certain poetic justice in that.''

Laney felt terribly sorry that Colombe hadn't been fortunate to meet a man as wonderful as Ben, who'd kept her from wallowing in self-pity and self-doubt and shown Laney how one-sided her relationship with Reese had been. She couldn't even manage any anger toward Colombe for trying to manipulate her into a jail cell. She, Colombe and Kristel had all been victimized by Reese/Patrick/Graham, whatever his real name was.

Colombe had just reacted violently and taken things to extremes.

"Colombe, I'm so sorry this has happened to you. To all three of us. I'm glad you told me. I think you needed to tell someone. But now you need to do the right thing and tell the police.'' Laney rose from the chair. Her heart pounded in her breast as she held out her hand to Colombe. "The wedding can be postponed. I'll come with you for moral support, okay?''

Colombe gritted her teeth fiercely. "I don't want your pity. I want you dead.''

Laney threw up her arms instinctively as Colombe looped the streamers of the bride's bouquet over her head and pulled them taut around her neck.

AT THE MINISTER'S SIGNAL, Josh and Scott blushed and strutted importantly down the red carpeted stairs to the bride's room located in the basement. Giving each other the thumbs-up sign, they tried to open the door to the room. It wouldn't budge.

"Mom, are you in there? It's us," Josh called, rattling the handle. The door was locked.

He heard a small crash.

"Mom? Colombe?" he repeated again, knocking real hard until his knuckles hurt. Josh looked at Scott and pressed his ear to the door. "She's not answering. But somebody's in there. I can hear them. They're making funny noises. What do you think that means?"

Scott frowned. "I dunno. Maybe she broke something and she's afraid she'll get in trouble. Or maybe the door's locked and she's climbing through the window 'cause she doesn't know how to open it. I'll go get Dad. He'll know what to do."

"Okay, I'll stay here. Hurry!" Josh pounded on the door again. "Mom? Can't you hear me? Open up!"

Ben heard his son's cries for help echo through the church. "Dad, come here quick! We've got a problem." Ben hadn't heard him raise his voice this high since before Rebecca's death.

Ben motioned for his brother Rob, the best man, to follow him. Heads swiveled and a ripple of concern swelled among the guests as they both ran down the aisle toward Scott.

"Mom won't open the door. I think she and Colombe are stuck in there." Scott rolled his eyes. "Girls!"

"Show me where," Ben ordered. He thundered down the stairs after Scott, wondering what the hell was going on.

Scott's explanation in no way prepared him for Josh's white expression as he whirled around at their approach.

"They're in here. I think they're having an argument."

Ben frowned in bewilderment and tried the door. "Laney?" Her lack of response and a muffled cry inside the room made hackles rise on the back of his neck. He turned to the boys, trying not to let his concern show. "Boys, go upstairs and tell Grandma I need the emergency tool kit from the trunk of her car. We can use a screwdriver to unlock the door. Hustle."

Ben signaled his brother to stay put and as soon as the boys were up the stairs, he and Rob kicked the door in. A horrible sense of déjà vu gripped his heart as he took in the chaos in the bride's room and the vicious expression on Colombe's face as she fought to squeeze the life out of Laney.

Ben flew across the room with his brother on his heels and clamped his hands around Colombe's wrists, crushing her wrists until she let go of the bouquet with a shriek that would stir the pigeons nesting in the bell tower. Ben wrestled her to the floor while Rob disentangled Laney from the ribbons cutting into her throat. Ben was amazed at Colombe's strength as she bucked and kicked at him. The woman was an Amazon.

He cast an anxious glance at Laney, who was redfaced and coughing. "Laney? Are you all right?" he demanded, still struggling with Colombe. "Rob, get Laney a chair. I think she's going to faint."

"I'm fine, Ben," Laney said weakly, though she allowed Rob to lead her to a chair. Her hands fluttered to her throat and she winced as she gently explored the extent of her injuries. "I didn't realize Colombe had locked the door. Did you tear your stitches?"

"I don't think so." The white marks on her neck made Ben see red. He tightened his grip on Colombe's wrists. "Do you mind telling me what's going on?"

Laney gave him a warning glance and shook her head. "In a minute. We have company."

Ben looked back over his shoulder and saw that she was right. A crowd had gathered outside the door now, including the minister. He could hear Scott and Josh's excited voices demanding to know what was going on, though he couldn't see them. Thank heavens his mother had them well in hand.

It took a few minutes to appoint Rob and another guest to take charge of Colombe, and to reassure the guests and the boys that everything was all right. Ben's heart turned to lead when Laney drew his mother aside and told her that they would let everyone know as soon as possible if the ceremony would be delayed or canceled altogether. Georgina took the boys upstairs, amid grumbling and protests.

Ben had a few protests of his own until Laney quietly informed him that Colombe had been Reese's first wife and had confessed to killing Reese. Grimfaced, Ben asked the minister if he could use the phone.

The arrest was made as discreetly as possible. Then

Ben went to find Laney, determined not to let Colombe cause her one more day of unhappiness.

LANEY SETTLED INTO a metal folding chair in the basement of the church and examined a section of torn cream-colored lace in her tea-length gown after she'd given her statement to the arresting officer.

It was over. Her wedding day had been the zoo she'd promised Colombe, and then some. Worse, the ceremony hadn't actually happened. Josh and Scott were probably very upset. The guests had probably all gone home. At least she could make sure the restaurant donated the meal to the food bank. They could try again another day.

She felt a warm hand settle on her shoulder. She looked up into Ben's heartbreaker blue-black eyes and felt cheated out of her wedding night in the Château Laurier with the prince of her dreams.

"How are you feeling?" he asked.

"Disappointed," she admitted ruefully.

"Me, too. And there are twenty people and a minister upstairs who are disappointed, too. Not to mention two little boys we know. They want you to know that if you're up to it, they'd still like a wedding to happen today. Otherwise, they'll all understand if you'd prefer for me to take you home. It's your call, sweetheart."

Laney rose and stood on tiptoe as Ben's arms circled her, pulling her against him. "It's not the romantic quiet little wedding I'd planned," she wailed into his chest. "My hair's a mess. Colombe tore my dress. My bouquet's been trampled…"

She felt the soothing balm of Ben's lips on her forehead.

"You look beautiful," he murmured, his warm breath tickling her temple. "There's no damage a little combing won't fix."

Laney shivered as he laid a trail of heated kisses from her cheek to her earlobe.

His voice, low and intimate, and, oh, so persuasive, caressed in her ear. "And who needs flowers? You smell like a tropical garden. Mom's probably got a sewing kit in her purse to take care of the tear in your dress."

Laney laughed at Ben's solutions to repairing the damage Colombe had done to their wedding. But, come to think of it, being rescued—a second time— by the man she loved was a hundred times more romantic than the illusion of romance she wanted to create with a perfect dress and flowers. Ben and the boys were perfect for her just the way they were. "Will you be this practical for the rest of our lives?"

Ben smiled and nuzzled the ultra-sensitive spot beneath her chin, making her knees quiver. "If I say yes, will you marry me and sleep with me tonight, Laney, my love?"

"Yes."

Ben grinned. "Yes."

Laney snared his firm chin and kissed him hard on the mouth, sighing with pleasure when his tongue stroked and teased and promised many more delights to come.

"I love you," she said fiercely, breathlessly, when she finally broke the kiss out of fear they might indiscreetly start the honeymoon right there in the base-ment. ''Send the boys down and tell the organist to start the music. I don't want to delay the wedding another minute. Oh, and ask your mother to act as the Matron of Honor.''

Only seconds later it seemed, music rang joyfully through the church. Contentment wrapped a gay bow around Laney's heart as she linked arms with Scott and Josh, who took their places on either side of her, faces beaming. When Laney's eyes locked with Ben's loving gaze as she took that first step down the aisle toward him and their life together, she knew she'd made the right, and only choice. After all they'd been through, it was time the Dobsons and the Forbeses became a family.

If you enjoyed what you just read,
then we've got an offer you can't resist!

Take 2 bestselling
love stories FREE!

Plus get a FREE surprise gift!

Clip this page and mail it to Harlequin Reader Service®

IN U.S.A.	**IN CANADA**
3010 Walden Ave.	P.O. Box 609
P.O. Box 1867	Fort Erie, Ontario
Buffalo, N.Y. 14240-1867	L2A 5X3

YES! Please send me 2 free Harlequin Intrigue® novels and my free surprise gift. Then send me 4 brand-new novels every month, which I will receive months before they're available in stores. In the U.S.A., bill me at the bargain price of $3.34 plus 25¢ delivery per book and applicable sales tax, if any*. In Canada, bill me at the bargain price of $3.71 plus 25¢ delivery per book and applicable taxes**. That's the complete price and a savings of over 10% off the cover prices—what a great deal! I understand that accepting the 2 free books and gift places me under no obligation ever to buy any books. I can always return a shipment and cancel at any time. Even if I never buy another book from Harlequin, the 2 free books and gift are mine to keep forever. So why not take us up on our invitation. You'll be glad you did!

181 HEN CNEZ
381 HEN CNE3

Name	(PLEASE PRINT)	
Address	Apt.#	
City	State/Prov.	Zip/Postal Code

* Terms and prices subject to change without notice. Sales tax applicable in N.Y.
** Canadian residents will be charged applicable provincial taxes and GST.
   All orders subject to approval. Offer limited to one per household.
   ® are registered trademarks of Harlequin Enterprises Limited.

INT99